UNCAGED KILLER!

As the tiger dropped smoothly to the ground, it spotted Frank. Its ears cocked forward, and its eyes locked on Frank's. It began inching slowly toward him, stalking him.

Frank knew he didn't have a prayer of outrunning or even dodging the huge predator.

Suddenly the animal stopped. Still staring at Frank, it went into a crouch, its hindquarters bunched up, its thick tail flicking and twitching.

Then it charged, accelerating to full speed instantly, its head level, ears flat, bone white fangs exposed— five hundred pounds of killer cat racing straight at him.

Books in THE HARDY BOYS CASEFILES™ Series

#1 DEAD ON TARGET	#75 NO WAY OUT
#2 EVIL, INC.	#76 TAGGED FOR TERROR
#3 CULT OF CRIME	#77 SURVIVAL RUN
#4 THE LAZARUS PLOT	#78 THE PACIFIC
#5 EDGE OF DESTRUCTION	CONSPIRACY
#6 THE CROWNING	#79 DANGER UNLIMITED
TERROR	#80 DEAD OF NIGHT
#7 DEATHGAME	#81 SHEER TERROR
#8 SEE NO EVIL	#82 POISONED PARADISE
#9 THE GENIUS THIEVES	#83 TOXIC REVENGE
#12 PERFECT GETAWAY	#84 FALSE ALARM
#13 THE BORGIA DAGGER	#85 WINNER TAKE ALL
#14 TOO MANY TRAITORS	#86 VIRTUAL VILLAINY
#29 THICK AS THIEVES	#87 DEAD MAN IN DEADWOOD
#30 THE DEADLIEST DARE	#88 INFERNO OF FEAR
#32 BLOOD MONEY	#89 DARKNESS FALLS
#33 COLLISION COURSE	#90 DEADLY ENGAGEMENT
#35 THE DEAD SEASON	#91 HOT WHEELS
#37 DANGER ZONE	#92 SABOTAGE AT SEA
#41 HIGHWAY ROBBERY	#93 MISSION: MAYHEM
#42 THE LAST LAUGH	#94 A TASTE FOR TERROR
#44 CASTLE FEAR	#95 ILLEGAL PROCEDURE
#45 IN SELF-DEFENSE	#96 AGAINST ALL ODDS
#46 FOUL PLAY	#97 PURE EVIL
#47 FLIGHT INTO DANGER	#98 MURDER BY MAGIC
#48 ROCK 'N' REVENGE	#99 FRAME-UP
#49 DIRTY DEEDS	#100 TRUE THRILLER
#50 POWER PLAY	#101 PEAK OF DANGER
#52 UNCIVIL WAR	#102 WRONG SIDE OF THE
#53 WEB OF HORROR	LAW
#54 DEEP TROUBLE	#103 CAMPAIGN OF CRIME
#55 BEYOND THE LAW	#104 WILD WHEELS
#56 HEIGHT OF DANGER	#105 LAW OF THE JUNGLE
#57 TERROR ON TRACK	#106 SHOCK JOCK
#60 DEADFALL	#107 FAST BREAK
#61 GRAVE DANGER	#108 BLOWN AWAY
#62 FINAL GAMBIT	#109 MOMENT OF TRUTH
#63 COLD SWEAT	#115 CAVE TRAP
#64 ENDANGERED SPECIES	#116 ACTING UP
#65 NO MERCY	#117 BLOOD SPORT
#66 THE PHOENIX	#118 THE LAST LEAP
EQUATION	#119 THE EMPEROR'S SHIELD
#69 MAYHEM IN MOTION	#120 SURVIVAL OF THE FITTEST
#71 REAL HORROR	#121 ABSOLUTE ZERO
#73 BAD RAP	#122 RIVER RATS
#74 ROAD PIRATES	#123 HIGH-WIRE ACT

Available from ARCHWAY Paperbacks

HIGH-WIRE ACT

FRANKLIN W. DIXON

AN ARCHWAY PAPERBACK
Published by POCKET BOOKS
New York London Toronto Sydney Tokyo Singapore

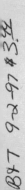

This book is a work of fiction. Names, characters, places and incidents are products of the author's imagination or are used fictitiously. Any resemblance to actual events or locales or persons, living or dead, is entirely coincidental.

AN ARCHWAY PAPERBACK *Original*

An Archway Paperback published by
POCKET BOOKS, a division of Simon & Schuster Inc.
1230 Avenue of the Americas, New York, NY 10020

ISBN: 0-671-56122-7

First Archway Paperback printing May 1997

10 9 8 7 6 5 4 3 2 1

THE HARDY BOYS, AN ARCHWAY PAPERBACK
and colophon are registered trademarks of Simon & Schuster Inc.

THE HARDY BOYS CASEFILES is a trademark
of Simon & Schuster Inc.

Printed in the U.S.A.

IL 6+

Chapter

1

"MOVE THAT WRECK!" an angry voice shouted.

"Move yours!" another voice shouted back.

"Can you believe this?" Frank Hardy asked his younger brother, Joe. "You'd think there was only one parking space at the whole circus."

A gleaming silver Jeep and a rusted yellow pickup were each angled partway into a grassy parking space. The two drivers were conducting a shouting match.

The Hardys had been cruising up and down the grassy lanes in their black van looking for a place to park. A few hundred yards ahead, a huge, red- and yellow-striped circus tent towered above the Bayport fairgrounds. It was a sunny Saturday afternoon, the first day of spring break.

1

Cars behind the Hardys' van began to honk.

"You came the wrong way," shouted the pickup driver, a skinny teenager wearing a baseball cap turned backward. He flung open his door and climbed out.

The guy in the Jeep, a burly man in a muscle T-shirt, jumped over his door to the ground.

"That kid's going to get eaten alive," Frank said. He opened his own door and got out. "Hey, fella! Easy, now," he said to the muscle man.

"Mind your own business," the man snapped as he moved toward the other driver.

But Frank stepped between the two drivers. "Look, everyone's here for a good time, right? Do you really want to spend the day at the police station because you got into a fight?"

"Well, he's not getting that space," the Jeep driver said, stabbing an index finger at the teen.

Just then a car pulled out of a spot two cars down.

The muscle man grunted, got back into his Jeep, and roared into the spot. The teen in the pickup pulled into the one he had been headed for all the time.

"Game over," Joe said as Frank got back into the van. "Nice way to start the afternoon. You think it's a sign of things to come?"

"I sure hope not," Frank said. They rode silently for another five minutes until they found a space at the far end of the parking area. Joe eased the van into the tight space, and the two brothers began the long walk to the big top.

"Can you believe how fast they set all this up?" Frank asked as they walked. "This field was empty yesterday." He squinted up at the thin, pointed red banners flapping in the wind sixty feet overhead. "It sure looks grubbier than I remember. Look how worn the canvas is."

"I still don't see why we had to rush," Joe said, checking his watch. "It's only two o'clock. The show doesn't start for an hour."

"Freddie said if we got here early, he'd show us around behind the scenes," Frank said.

Frank and Joe were glad to have a week off from school. Visiting the Nicholson Brothers Circus seemed like a good way to start the break, especially since Freddie Felix, a Bayport High School graduate, now worked with the show.

"A personal tour *would* be cool," Joe admitted. "I can't remember the last time I was at a circus."

"Mom and Dad brought us," Frank said. "You were scared of the clowns."

"Yeah, right," Joe said.

"You probably buried it in your memory because it was so traumatic," Frank continued, stifling a grin. "If I remember correctly, you had to be carried out of the tent because you were making such a racket."

Joe socked his brother's shoulder, shutting him up. "Tell me about Freddie," he said, changing

3

the subject. "He was a year ahead of you, right? Did you know him well?"

"Well enough to know he was hilarious. A major class clown. He was really talented, too."

"He'd have to be. Going from class clown to being a paid circus pro is no simple feat," Joe said. "Hey, there's the rest of the gang," he added, looking toward the circus entrance.

Standing at the big top was Callie Shaw, Frank's girlfriend. Vanessa Bender, Joe's girlfriend, stood next to her, along with Chet Morton, a good friend of both Hardys, who was just polishing off an ice-cream cone.

"Hi, guys," Vanessa called as Frank and Joe approached. Callie flashed Frank a smile and he gave her a quick kiss.

As they walked toward the big top, Chet said, "This should be cool, seeing someone we know. I wonder what Freddie had to do to become a clown, anyway?"

"Well, for starters, he went to clown school," Frank said.

"Clown school?" Vanessa said. "What do you do in clown school, *clown* around?" She looked at Callie and began to laugh.

"Yes! And it's the only school where teachers make you crack jokes in class," Callie said.

"And you have to laugh during assemblies," Chet said, joining in, "or else you get detention."

"I wonder what their exams are like," Frank said, laughing at the possibilities.

"Pie throwing," Joe said. "I'm sure you have to throw a pie in your neighbor's face."

"Or bash someone on the head with a rubber hammer," Callie cracked, her brown eyes flashing.

"Yeah, and for homework you walk around in those huge shoes," Chet said.

"I wonder if anyone ever flunks out," Vanessa said.

"Imagine flunking out of clown school for being too serious," Callie said. She looked at Vanessa, and the two friends exploded with laughter.

"I don't think I want you two to sit next to each other during the circus," Frank said, putting his arm around Callie.

The five friends joined the crowd of people milling about the fairgrounds. Young children clutched cotton candy and dripping ice-cream cones as they walked happily among the concession stands, eager for the show to start.

"How are you going to find Freddie?" Callie asked.

Frank noticed a tall figure standing alone between a pair of trailers with his back to them. He wore a bright yellow jacket with orange polka dots, and baggy red plaid pants. A tiny silver derby sat at an angle on his curly green wig.

"I'll see if he knows," Frank said, moving toward the clown. "Excuse me."

The big man turned, and Frank noticed he was holding a smoldering cigar in his hand.

"I'm looking for Freddie Felix," Frank said. "He's a clown."

The clown pointed the thick cigar toward the big top.

"Thanks," Frank said.

As the group headed toward the tent, they passed a concession stand. "Hold on," Chet said. "I want to get a caramel apple. Anyone else want anything?"

"I could go for some cotton candy," Callie said. "Vanessa?"

"Definitely."

"I'll pass for now," Frank said.

"Hey, we'll meet you guys in the seats, okay?" Joe asked. "Sit close to the entrance so we can find you."

Around the huge, brightly striped tent, Frank and Joe found an entrance with a yellow silk rope across it. A sign said No Admittance.

"We're here to see one of the clowns," Frank said to the circus employee sitting at the entrance. The man lifted the rope and waved the Hardys inside.

"This is like having a backstage pass," Joe said as they entered the enormous tent.

Inside, a woman on a unicycle juggled tennis balls, while a man in a tuxedo and top hat tapped a hand-held mike. "Ladies and gentlemen," he said. The mike let out a loud, electronic squeal.

Frank saw three clowns standing near a pair of tall, gleaming metal poles with a thin wire stretched between them. "There's Freddie," he said, pointing to the one who was short, thin, and slightly built.

Freddie Felix wore a huge orange beret that drooped over his face like a deflated basketball, a bright red shirt, too-short green pants with knee patches, and black makeup on his jaw that was supposed to look like a hobo's five o'clock shadow.

"Freddie!" Frank called as he and Joe trotted over.

"Frank Hardy," Freddie said as he slapped Frank on the back. "How's it going?"

"Not too bad," Frank said, reaching out to shake the clown's hand. No sooner had Frank grasped the hand than Freddie let out a banshee cry and yanked his arm away, leaving a startled Frank holding the limp, rubber, and very fake hand.

Freddie chuckled as he took the rubber prop back. "Sorry," he said, "but that *is* what they pay me to do around here."

"You almost had me." Frank shook his head and smiled. "Do you know my brother, Joe?"

"Hey, Joe," Freddie said. The younger Hardy shook the clown's hand cautiously.

"So, how's life under the big top?" Frank asked.

"The best. Doesn't every kid dream of running away to join the circus?"

"Not every kid," Joe said. "I wanted to be a major-league baseball player."

"Well, Freddie actually became what he always dreamed of. Unlike you," Frank teased Joe. He turned to his friend. "And you're not just cleaning up after the elephants."

"Nah," Freddie said, grinning. "That takes special training. Actually, we'll hire anyone we can get to do that job. The turnover's highest among the laborers."

"Laborers?" Joe asked.

"The workers—the guys who do the grunt work. They're the ones who carry things in and out of the rings between acts—the sword swallower's swords, the elephants' pedestals, sections of the cat cage. The turnover's high because the work's hard and the pay is peanuts. It's great free transportation, though. Just sign on with a traveling show, and six weeks later you're somewhere else and you've been paid to get there."

"So, what is it like being a clown?" Frank asked.

"I love it. I'm still just at the bottom of the clown ladder. White-face clowns are at the top. A few rungs down are the character clowns like me, you know, the ones that look like hobos."

"Well, your clown face looks pretty good," Joe said, eyeing the red stars on Freddie's cheeks.

"It's registered, you know. All clown faces are.

Another clown can copy your clothes and even your act, but never your face. You send a photo of it to the Clown and Character Registry, where they paint it on a goose egg and store it for safekeeping."

"A goose egg?" Joe asked. "No kidding."

"It's a tradition from the 1500s. Clowns painted their faces on goose eggs so they could remember the faces they used when they wanted to paint them on again.

"Not that the job's all fun and games," Freddie continued. "You've got to be in top shape and have great timing, reflexes, and coordination."

As he spoke, Freddie leaned back toward the high-wire pole—and missed. As he spun around, arms flailing, Frank and Joe both reached to grab him, but he slipped between their hands and fell flat on his face. The next instant, he was on his feet again, grinning.

"Nice move," Joe said.

Freddie stood, swatting dust from his costume. "Just a little something I learned in clown school, along with tightrope-walking, juggling, and squeezing into a subcompact car with six other clowns."

"You must do a lot of practicing," Frank said.

"Absolutely," Freddie said. "Even the screwups in our act are planned and rehearsed, both to give the audience the best show and for safety's sake. We're about to do a final rehearsal now. Want to watch?"

"You bet," Frank said.

"You don't use a net during rehearsal?" Joe asked.

Freddie shook his head. "That's the setup crew's fault. They're usually behind and don't get the safety net up until just before the actual show. But this routine's stock. It's almost as safe as performing it on the ground."

After positioning the Hardys where they'd have a good view, Freddie climbed a chain ladder to a tiny platform twenty-five feet above the hard-packed ground. Another clown, in black- and green-striped coveralls and a blue wig, was already waiting up above. The second clown edged out onto the wire, making a taut V of the cable, and Freddie followed. Meanwhile a third clown, wearing a silver-studded black leather motorcycle jacket, helmet, and funny-looking big white gloves, started out from the opposite platform.

Holding an eight-foot metal tube as a balance pole, Freddie edged out slowly. The other two, meeting at the middle of the wire, began a mock argument about being in each other's way. They shouted, and each time they waved their hands, the wire bounced, making Freddie seem about to fall. He leaned far forward, then far backward, windmilling his free arm and regaining his balance just in time.

"He's good," Joe said, and Frank nodded. Not

even some of the best athletes they'd seen had as a good sense of balance.

Finally Freddie tapped the clown closer to him on the shoulder and signaled that he wanted to pass. But the biker clown drew a red-and-white juggling pin from his baggy pocket. Holding it behind his back in his huge, floppy, white-gloved hand, he also tapped the second clown on the shoulder. As that clown turned, the biker clown swung the pin at his head. The clown in the middle ducked, and the pin hit Freddie instead. Frank and Joe chuckled.

Freddie jerked upright and tottered as if dazed. The Hardys shook their heads, smiling, but then the pole slipped from Freddie's hands. It dropped straight down, clanging loudly on the ground. Freddie continued to sway on the wire.

"Wait a second," Frank said, staring open-mouthed up at the wire. "He's not kidding this time." As Frank spoke, Freddie pitched forward and toppled off the wire, soaring headfirst toward the ground twenty-five feet below.

Chapter

2

As Freddie plummeted to the ground, Frank raced to try to break his friend's fall, reaching him at the last possible instant. Frank took a hard glancing blow, and his chest hit the ground, knocking the air out of him. Freddie crashed to the ground in a heap on Frank, then rolled off him, hitting his head hard on the ground.

"Frank, Freddie!" Joe cried, rushing to the pair. "You okay?"

Frank blinked and sat up. "Yeah. I feel as if I've just been tackled, but I think I'm all right. What about Freddie?"

Joe kneeled over the fallen clown. "He took a pretty bad blow to the head." Freddie lay on his back, perfectly still. Joe put his ear to Freddie's chest. "Frank, he's not breathing."

Quickly, Joe checked his pulse. "Nothing," he said grimly.

"Call an ambulance," Frank shouted to the ringmaster, who had seen it all. The man raced out of the tent.

"He needs CPR," Joe said. He tilted Freddie's head back, pinched the clown's nostrils closed, then blew two short, forceful puffs into his mouth, watching to see if his chest rose.

"I'll do chest compressions," Frank said. He put the heel of his hand just above Freddie's lowest ribs and started pumping up and down, hoping to jump-start his friend's heart.

Soon they heard a siren, and within a couple of minutes an ambulance, its lights flashing, rolled in through a flap someone had opened in the side of the tent. A small crowd had gathered.

Two white-jacketed paramedics leaped out. When they heard the Hardys' account of what had happened, the taller one said, "Let's get him to the ER right away. You guys can hop in if you like and get a ride to the hospital with your friend here."

They quickly and carefully lifted Freddie onto a stretcher and into the ambulance. One of the paramedics continued CPR with a bag-valve mask while the other drove, siren wailing, to the hospital.

* * *

13

An hour later the Hardys sat in the waiting room at Bayport General Hospital. Freddie's parents and sister had arrived and were waiting as the doctors took MRIs—fine-tuned X rays—of his head and neck, checking for damage to the brain or spinal column.

Frank called the Shaw home and left a message for Callie on the answering machine, telling her where he and Joe were. It was a system he and Callie had arranged to use in emergencies. Frank knew that when he and Joe didn't meet Callie, Vanessa, and Chet at the seats, Callie would call the machine and retrieve the message.

When Frank returned to the waiting area, he saw Mrs. Felix dabbing her eyes with a handkerchief while her daughter sat with her arm around her. Mr. Felix, short and thin, paced back and forth and looked up every time someone passed.

"Why aren't they telling us anything?" he said.

"Dad, I'm sure they'll come out when they have something to say," Freddie's sister told him.

Catching Joe's eye, Frank shook his head. Waiting was always hard on a family.

A tall, lanky man in a doctor's coat appeared at the swinging door that separated the waiting area from the emergency room. In his early fifties, the man wore wire-framed glasses and a neatly trimmed gray beard, and he moved energetically. "Mr. and Mrs. Felix?" he asked.

The concerned parents stood.

"How is he, Doctor?" Mr. Felix asked.

"The good news is his MRI shows no skull fracture." The doctor nodded toward Frank. "From what the paramedics told me, you have that young man to thank. By breaking your son's fall, he very likely saved his life."

The entire Felix family turned to look gratefully at Frank.

"Unfortunately," the doctor continued, "we can't be sure how extensive the injuries are. Your son has a subdural hematoma, the equivalent of a deep bruise on the brain. We're draining the blood to relieve intracranial pressure, but Frederick's in a coma, and the truth is, we don't know when he'll come out of it."

The doctor sighed and shook his head. "All we can do is monitor him closely. We're going to move him to intensive care and continue some tests. We'll keep you posted if there's any change whatsoever."

"Thanks, Doctor," Mr. Felix said. Then he turned to console his wife.

"Come on, Joe," Frank whispered. "Let's give them some privacy." But as Frank and Joe moved toward the door, Mrs. Felix called, "Wait, Frank."

She came and took his hand. "We can never thank you enough. Freddie's accident might have been even worse if it weren't for you. You put yourself in danger, and you could have been hurt badly."

"Anyone would have done the same, Mrs.

Felix," Frank said. He turned to Freddie's father. "Please let us know if there's anything else we can do."

They said their goodbyes to Freddie's family and caught a taxi back out to the fairgrounds, discussing Freddie's fall on the way back.

"Joe, I just keep replaying the scene in my mind, watching him pitch off that wire," Frank said. "How could it have happened? He seemed so sure of himself."

"It was right after he got whacked with that juggling pin," Joe said. "But that must have been part of the performance, don't you think?"

Frank shook his head and shrugged.

When they reached the fairgrounds, the Hardys found that the show had ended and the crowds had left the tent. Work crews in red coveralls were loading the trucks. A note from Callie on the Hardys' windshield let them know she had received Frank's message and that they all wished Freddie well.

"Hey, isn't that Con over there?" Joe said.

Outside the big top sat a pair of Bayport police cruisers. Spotting their longtime friend, Officer Con Riley, Frank and Joe beelined toward him.

"What's up, fellas?" Riley asked. "Were you here for the show?"

"I'll say," Frank said. "If you're here about the Freddy Felix accident, we saw it happen. In fact, we had front-row seats. We're just coming back from the ER."

After the Hardys described the accident and Freddie's condition, Con shook his head. "A real shame. It's got to be tough on the parents."

Con tapped his clipboard with his pen. "I've been talking with a few witnesses for my report. They say the clowns were rehearsing on the high wire when Tiny Winston—he's the clown in the motorcyle getup—swung a juggling pin at the clown in stripes, Jonesie Hobson. Hobson ducked, and that's when Felix got hit and fell."

"That's pretty much it," Frank said.

"Except for one thing," Con said. "Wait until you see this."

Con moved to the police car and took a juggling pin from the seat. "This is the pin he was hit with," he said, handing it to Frank.

Frank hefted it. "This thing's heavy. How could getting hit with this be part of the act?"

"It wasn't," Con said. "The pin that's supposed to be used is called a breakaway, a prop pin that looks and feels real but breaks apart on impact. Unfortunately this pin was used instead."

"What does that mean?" Joe asked, looking from Frank to Con. "Foul play?"

"Too soon to tell," Con said. "Winston says he took the pin from the place where the breakaway is kept, on top of the prop box. But when he hit Felix today . . . well, you know the rest."

"Couldn't Winston tell by the look or feel of it that it wasn't the prop pin?" Frank asked.

"He says the pins look and feel almost identi-

17

cal, especially if you're wearing gloves, which he was. Then you can't feel the seam where it breaks away."

"Who was in charge of setting the pin on the prop box?" Frank asked.

"That's the funny part. Your friend Felix himself," Con said. "He always brings it from his trailer about an hour beforehand." Con shook his head. "Could be today he grabbed the wrong one. It sounds like an unfortunate mixup to me."

Con flipped his notebook closed and slipped his pen into his pocket. "Let's just be glad he wasn't killed."

A sergeant came up. "You about done here, Riley? We just got another call."

"Right, Sarge," Con said, moving to his car. "See you around, guys," he said to Frank and Joe.

"Yeah," Joe said.

"Later, Con," Frank added, nodding.

After the cruisers left, Frank stood with the red-and-white pin in hand.

"We'd better get going, too," Joe said.

But Frank just kept standing there, weighing the pin. His face was troubled.

"Frank?" Joe said.

"Joe," his older brother finally said. "There's something about this that bothers me. I mean, Freddie seemed too conscientious for something like this to happen. From the way he was talking, I don't think he would ever be that careless."

"I agree," Joe said. "You think someone switched pins by accident—or on purpose?"

"I think we should check it out, see if we can find out if anyone had anything to gain by hurting Freddie—or even killing him."

"Let's look at it from all angles," Joe said. "Maybe he meant to grab one pin but he grabbed another. Accidents happen."

"Maybe. Maybe not," Frank said.

"Hey, aren't we forgetting one small detail?" Joe gestured to the men in red, busily lowering tent poles and heavy spotlights, rolling huge sections of canvas, and lifting thick coils of electric cable onto idling trucks. "The show is leaving. Another few hours and this'll all be gone."

"Well," Frank said, "we could always join up for a few days."

"What?"

"Come on, Joe," Frank said. "You didn't have any plans for spring break anyway, did you? We sign on as workers and investigate along the way."

"Earth to Frank. Come in, Frank," Joe said. "That sounds crazy—like something I'd dream up."

"Joe, I just keep picturing Freddie there in a hospital bed, his family not knowing whether he'll live or die. He's a good kid, and he could be in a coma the rest of his life. The very least we could do is try to find out what happened."

"Well, since you put it that way," Joe said. "But we don't even know if they're hiring."

"You heard what Freddie said. There's a constant turnover among the workers. I'll bet we'd get hired on the spot."

"And I'll bet I know what job we'd get hired to do," Joe said with a slow chuckle. He turned to look at a few workers who were lowering a tent pole a few yards away. "We'll get to shovel—"

Suddenly the forty-foot pole slipped its rigging. The thick line that two men were holding suddenly went slack, and the men tumbled backward to the ground.

"Watch it!" shouted a third man.

Joe saw the huge pole swinging free—and coming right at Frank.

Chapter

3

"FRANK!" JOE LUNGED at his brother and shoved him hard with both hands, knocking him backward onto the ground. The huge pole flew past the spot where Frank had been standing a split second before, then hit the dirt with a loud thud.

"Man," Frank said. "Do I look like a punching bag? Couldn't you have just told me to get out of the way?" He got to his feet and brushed off his clothing.

"Better safe than sorry," Joe said. "I thought you'd rather have *me* knock you over than a tent pole," Joe said.

"You guys all right?" Several men rushed up, all of them in red coveralls.

"Yeah, we're okay," Frank said.

"Well, you shouldn't be back here," one of the men said as the group went back to work.

"See?" Joe said. "Circuses are dangerous." He gestured toward the workers pushing carts, hauling canvas, and loading heavy equipment. "Add in all the wild animals and stunts, and there's bound to be accidents."

"Fine," Frank shot back. "Then if it was an accident with Freddie, we should be able to confirm that fast. But I'm telling you my hunch is it wasn't. I'll bet Freddie triple-checked his props, and regardless of what Con and the police think, I'm not ready to write this off yet. If Freddie left the prop pin unattended for an hour, anyone could have made a switch. Besides, I don't think it's just a matter of *if*. I think we ought to be asking *why*."

"Okay," Joe said, "you've got a point, but what about all the people who saw us with Freddie already?"

"Easy. We just say we came backstage to ask him about joining up. We knew that one of our hometown boys had joined the circus, and we got bitten by the circus bug, too," Frank said. "It's our once-in-a-lifetime opportunity."

"You've convinced me," Joe said. "Maybe it wasn't my dream, but it sounds like the way to find out what happened to Freddie."

"I saw a trailer back there that said Office on it," Frank said. "Let's apply right now."

As things turned out, getting hired proved

easy. With the high turnover Freddie had mentioned, the application process was practically nonexistent. Mickey Barnes, the short, stocky show boss, sat behind a cluttered desk covered with the overflowing ashtrays of a chain-smoker.

"Brothers, huh?" he said. "Well, you both look like you can handle the work. And you're over sixteen, right?"

"Yes, sir," Frank said.

Barnes fished two application forms from a drawer, gave Frank and Joe pencils, and, as they wrote, explained that the pay was one hundred dollars a week plus bed and board.

As Barnes collected the forms and dropped them into a drawer, he said, "Go find Gus. He's our foreman. He'll give you your monkey suits."

"You mean those red coveralls?" Joe asked.

But the boss only waved his hand and went back to his paperwork.

The Hardys found Gus outside the big top. He turned out to be about forty, stubble jawed and rail thin.

"New workers, eh?" he asked, squinting at them. "Well, come on," he said, and crooked a finger for Frank and Joe to follow.

After giving them their bright red coveralls with the circus name stitched in gold across the back, Gus led them across the lot. He explained that the Nicholson Brothers Circus staged two shows a day in each town along its travel route, and after the last show each night, the workers packed up. Then the forty-vehicle caravan of cars, trucks, RVs, and trailers drove through the night to the next town to set up all over again in the morning.

"You ever see those red cardboard arrows taped to highway signs?" Gus asked. "That's us. Our lead car leaves them as directions for the rest. Now watch your step here." He had led them to a dilapidated red semitrailer with a sliding side door. "This is where you sleep," he said.

Frank and Joe followed him up a splintery, three-step wooden ladder into a large, gloomy interior with just two small windows. The smell of sweat and cigarette smoke assaulted them, and Joe, catching Frank's eye, waved his hand beneath his nose. About thirty triple-decker bunks were nailed to the walls. Some had grimy jeans, beat-up boots, or old sneakers thrown across them, showing they'd been claimed.

Gus pointed to a pair of empty bunks, a middle one and a bottom one. The lower one was just inches off the dusty floor. "Those are yours," the foreman said. Each had a lumpy-looking two-inch-thick mattress and a threadbare blanket. Gus turned to lead them out but then paused to add, "Better keep your valuables with you, if you got any."

The rest of the evening, as the show packed up, the Hardys were free to walk around in their monkey suits, as Barnes had called them. Gus said that since it was their first day, they didn't have to work but should just try to absorb as much as they could and lend a hand if necessary.

Frank didn't want to waste time, though. The minute he and Joe were alone, he said, "This may be the most free time we get. Let's use it."

So when they saw Mickey Barnes walking hurriedly from his trailer holding some papers, the Hardys intercepted him.

"Hi, Mr. Barnes," Frank said.

"What's up, fellas?" Barnes answered, barely looking their way and not breaking stride.

"Um, we were wondering," Frank began as he and Joe fell into step beside the show boss, "will you be needing a clown to fill in for that one we heard got hurt? Because my brother and I—"

"Forget it, fellas," Barnes said. "That's not how it works. I got clowns sending me their résumés and clown-school diplomas every day. There are more clowns than jobs."

He stopped and looked at Frank and Joe as if for the first time. "You don't just walk into a clown job," he said gruffly. "The field's tight. You've got to know juggling, makeup, high wire—and only the best get full-time work. I got part-timers who'd kill for a full-time slot."

Joe wondered if anyone actually did kill to get closer to a full-time slot. "How many part-timers are with the show now?" he asked.

"Tiny Winston, Sonny Bones," Barnes said. "No, wait—Sonny's in Sarasota, working on a seal act. Of course, there *was* Freddie Felix, but

25

he's out now." Suddenly Barnes stopped in his tracks. "Now, if you're about done asking questions—"

"Yes, sir," Frank said. "And thanks for your time."

As the boss hurried off, Joe said, "You heard that. He has clowns who'd kill for a full-time slot."

"I think that was just an expression," Frank said. "But you do have a point there."

"And Tiny Winston, the clown who actually walloped Freddie," Joe continued, "Barnes just said he's a part-timer. Even though Freddie was a part-timer, too, with him out of the way, it gets someone like Tiny one step closer to a full-time job."

"That's a pretty clear motive," Frank said.

Frank and Joe headed off to find Winston but detoured first past the office-trailer to use Mickey Barnes's cell phone. The door stood open, so they went in.

Calling home, Frank got the answering machine. "They're probably catching dinner and a movie," he said to Joe, holding his hand over the mouthpiece. At the beep, Frank said, "Hi, Mom and Dad. Joe and I are working a case that came up suddenly. We might be gone a couple of days, but don't worry. We'll be in touch and fill you in on everything. As always, we'll be careful. Oh— could one of you pick up the van? It's at the fairgrounds," he added before clicking off.

Frank and Joe found Winston outside the big top practicing his juggling. He was using five oranges and an apple and was taking bites of the apple each time it came around. When only the core was left, he tossed the apple aside and caught the oranges in a bag.

Frank and Joe stood in awe, watching the skilled clown. "Tiny Winston, right?" Frank said when Tiny was finished.

Seeing Frank and Joe in coveralls, the clown said, "I remember you two. You were talking to Freddie Felix. So, you decided to get a taste of show business, eh?"

"We thought it'd be something different for a while," Frank said.

"It's different, all right. I guess circuses will always draw them in. It's like that joke about the guy who gets a job cleaning up after the elephants. Somebody says, 'That job looks terrible. It's dirty, you probably don't make much money, people must treat you bad.' 'Yup,' the guy says. 'All true.' 'So why don't you quit?' the other asks. 'What?' he says. 'And give up show business?' "

The clown shook his head. "People'll always be running off to join circuses as long as there's a single circus to run off to."

"Have you been with the show long?" Joe asked.

"Four months. I signed on in Georgia as a character clown."

27

"Really?" Frank said. "So now that Freddie's gone I guess you move up a slot?"

"Now, hold on just a second. I've already been through this with the cops," Winston said. "If you think I had anything to do with that pin being substituted you're dead wrong. Freddie's a friend of mine, a real nice guy. I hope he's okay. Of course, I feel awful since I'm the one who hit him.

"That pin was where the breakaway's supposed to be. I grabbed it, just like I always do. I know it looks bad, since he had seniority and I was part time and it cuts my competition for a full-time job. I told the cops all this. Hey, full-time job or not, I'd never hurt another clown just so I had a chance at an opening," Winston said, seeming genuinely indignant. "And even if I would, why would I do something so obvious? Like I said, I was surprised he made a mistake like that—taking out the wrong pin. He's always so careful. I tell you what I think. I think he was distracted by the falling-out he had with Darbar. His mind was somewhere else."

"Who's Darbar?" Frank asked.

"They had a big run-in yesterday—or I should say Darbar was yelling at Freddie. I don't know what about."

A worker came up and interrupted them.

"You're the new guys, right?" he asked the Hardys. The man was older; he was short and had thin brown hair. "Gus says to come help load Queen Sasha's fans."

"That's the trained-horse act," Winston explained. "Sasha uses these four huge fans to blow confetti around like a snowstorm. She rides through it doing ballet poses."

"It makes a real mess, too," said the worker, turning to leave.

"See you around, Tiny," Frank said as he and Joe followed.

"You fellas take care," Tiny said.

As Frank and Joe walked a half dozen or so paces behind the worker, Frank said in a low voice, "So, what do you think?"

"I think Tiny's next in line for a job now that Freddie's out of the picture," Joe said. "It's a motive, but you heard what he said. He'd have to be crazy to think he could get away with it in front of so many witnesses."

"Just the opposite," Frank said. "That's the beauty of it. The police bought his story about the mix-up, didn't they? And even if they did think the prop-swap was intentional, they'd still have to prove he did it."

"Whatever," Joe said. "Let's find out who this Darbar is and go talk to him."

"Or her," Frank said.

First Frank and Joe had to help load the fans— four tall, big-bladed, free-standing contraptions that looked like bigger versions of the fans in old banks and libraries that didn't have air conditioning.

Queen Sasha turned out to be thin, blond, and fifty or so, with a gravelly voice. "Hurry up," she snapped as Frank and Joe worked. "And be careful! That's expensive equipment."

"That's a performer for you," one of the workers muttered to Joe. "She acts like she's too good for us."

When they finished, Gus found plenty of other chores to keep the Hardys busy.

"So much for just watching," Joe muttered to Frank.

Before long it was time for the forty vehicles to take to the highway, and Frank and Joe headed for the semi.

"We'll have to save Darbar for tomorrow," Frank said.

In his bunk, Joe couldn't fall asleep. Lying in the dark with two dozen strangers snoring around him, clinking bottles rolling around the floor, and someone's hissing transistor radio a few bunks away, he tossed and turned miserably.

It wasn't until the sun was beginning to rise that the rocking of the truck, the hum of the highway, and the lateness of the hour caught up with him, and he finally drifted off.

The semi's door slid open with a screech, and Frank blinked his eyes at the gray morning light. Rising on one elbow, he saw a wide field overgrown with weeds and a thick woods beyond. Off to the left was a parking lot with cracked gray asphalt and faded yellow parking lines.

"Everybody up! Let's go!"

Gus was propping the ladder beneath the doorway. "Time to go to work," he called. Then he was gone.

Frank squinted at his wristwatch: six-fifteen. Others stirred in the gloom. Men coughed, wheezed, grunted, and muttered to themselves as they stretched and began to dress.

Frank leaned over the edge of his bunk. "Hey, Joe, how'd you sleep?"

The younger Hardy looked up, scowling. Frank thought his brother's face looked like something from a badly carved totem pole.

"I think I got about two hours' worth," Joe said. "This mattress feels as if it has golf balls in it."

Frank swung his feet over the edge and dropped to the splintery floor. "A few days' work and I'll bet we'll be ready to sleep standing up."

Joe stood up slowly and rubbed the back of his neck. "That's just great. I love having something to look forward to," he muttered.

After their morning duties, the Hardys ate breakfast under the small, open-sided red-and-white tent everyone called the chow tent.

The workers sat at three long wooden tables, not talking but hunched over their plates, shoveling up fried eggs with burned shards of toast. They paused only long enough to take huge gulps of steaming black coffee.

"Anyone know who Darbar is?" Frank asked, taking up his fork. It had a bit of dried egg across the tines and he picked it off with his fingernail.

No one answered.

"Darbar," Joe said. "We're trying to find out who that is."

A man across the table—a hulk of a man with the fattest neck Joe had ever seen—stopped chewing and stared at Joe. But before he could speak, another guy down the table grunted, "That'd be Sinjay Darbar."

The Hardys turned toward the voice.

A small, thin man, about sixty, with one eye that was half shut but looked almost white between the lids, snorted loudly, turned his head, and spat onto the dirt. "Darbar's the snake charmer," the man said. "He's in that red-and-green trailer out near the cat tent."

After Frank and Joe had finished breakfast, Frank said, "Let's head over and find out what that argument with Freddie was all about."

But at Darbar's trailer no one answered their knock.

"Wonder when he'll be back," Frank said.

Standing on the top step, Joe glanced in the trailer window.

On a small couch lay an attractive young woman in her late teens or early twenties, who appeared to be asleep. She wore a white sari and had a dot in the middle of her forehead.

Joe quickly scanned the room to see if anyone else was there. When he glanced back at the young woman, he gasped.

A gray snake was now slithering along the pink bedspread toward the young woman's face. The hooded reptile's mouth was open, its forked tongue was flicking, and its fangs were bared as it went for her throat.

Chapter

4

Joe kicked the door to the trailer with all his strength. The flimsy door burst open, and he rushed inside as the young woman sat up, blinking her eyes.

Snatching up an umbrella he spotted beside the door, Joe lunged forward, slipping the handle underneath the snake. He raised it quickly and, snatching the knob of what he hoped was a closet, yanked the door open, flung the snake inside, then slammed the door shut.

"Are you all right?" Joe asked the young woman as she stared, wide-eyed.

Before she could say a word, a voice sounded behind Joe. "How dare you? What are you doing in my trailer?"

Joe spun. Frank, who had followed Joe in, also turned, and saw a man in a turban standing at the doorway of the next room. He looked about fifty and wore baggy cotton pants and a collarless buttoned shirt. "Who are you?" he demanded. "What right have you to break into my home?"

"I saw that snake through the window," Joe said. "It was about to—"

"Father," the young woman interrupted. "Don't you see? He thought I was in danger. He was trying to help me." She turned to Joe and smiled. "Isn't that so?"

"Of course," Joe said. "I saw you asleep, and I figured the snake must have escaped from somewhere."

The Indian man moved to the closet. "I only hope for your sake you have not hurt Rosmali." He reached in and took the snake out, cradling it with both hands. "There, my little flower," the man said soothingly. He raised the creature to his face and looked into its eyes. "Are you all right?"

The reptile's tongue darted.

"Um, what kind of snake is that?" Frank asked, backing up a step.

"Rosmali is an Indian cobra," the young woman said.

"They're not poisonous or anything, are they?" Joe asked.

"Extremely," the young woman said. "Rosie is quite used to us, though, and Father drains her poison sacs often." She extended her hand to Joe. "My name is Shahela, and this is my father, Sinjay Darbar." Joe shook Shahela's hand. "What is your name?"

"Joe Hardy. And this is my brother, Frank. We just started yesterday."

"I knew I had not seen you before," Shahela said.

Sinjay Darbar, who had continued comforting his pet, now turned and demanded, "What are you doing here anyway?"

"Well," Frank said, thinking fast, "we heard you had an argument with Freddie Felix yesterday, um, and since we're new, we didn't want to do anything that might annoy you. So we thought we'd stop by and see what it was about."

Frank shot Joe a look. The older Hardy knew it sounded like a lame excuse, but it was all he could come up with. The two brothers waited to see if Darbar would buy it.

The snake charmer scowled. "Freddie Felix. That impudent dog."

"You probably heard he got hurt yesterday," Frank said.

"And I'm not sorry in the least. He got what was coming to him."

"Oh, Father," Shahela objected.

"Shahela, silence. Remember your upbringing," her father ordered. "Show your elders the proper respect."

"Do you know Freddie well?" Frank asked.

"Well enough," Darbar said angrily. "And I have had more than enough of your questions. You have no business harassing the performers. I can see from your uniforms you are just workers. Well, I will talk to Mickey Barnes. He will remind you of your proper place. Now, leave my trailer at once."

As the Hardys stepped from the trailer, Darbar slammed the door behind them.

"Man," Joe said as he and Frank walked away. "Just try doing a favor for some people."

"We'd better get back to work," Frank said. "I think we've asked enough questions for now. If Darbar complains, we could wind up getting fired, and that would bring this investigation to a grinding halt."

"Right now that doesn't sound like such a bad thing," Joe said. "But of course it would mean we'd have to find our own way home. I don't even know what town we're in."

"I vote we go right to the heart of this investigation: Freddie's trailer. If something about him made someone want to kill him, there could be clues there."

They found Freddie's trailer locked, but after a few moments' work with the small, trusty picks he kept in his wallet, Joe swung the door open.

The young clown's tiny trailer turned out to be hardly bigger than its single bed.

"He probably scraped together every penny he had to buy this place and that rusty old clunker he pulls it with," Joe said, describing Freddie's dented, faded, ten-year-old green subcompact. Even though Freddie had been injured, his vehicle stayed with the circus. One of the other clowns had driven it from Bayport the night before.

"I don't think a part-time clown's salary goes far," Frank said.

The room held little more than the bed, a small chest of drawers, and a tiny refrigerator. Freddie's framed clown school diploma hung on the wall above a shelf filled with books on juggling, clown makeup, and the history of the circus. Beneath a small mirror, jars of makeup stood in neat rows. A cardboard carton contained rubber juggling balls and rings, big floppy shoes, a mock football jersey, and props that included a rubber hatchet, oversize boxing gloves, and assorted wigs and foam-rubber noses.

"Everything he needed," Frank said as he looked the place over.

"Hey, check this out," Joe said.

The younger Hardy stood in front of the makeup table. Tucked into the edges of the mirror were postcards from cities the circus had visited. There was also a photo. The Hardys recognized Freddie in his clown costume standing beside a short, slightly built, fortyish man with a thin mustache and glasses. The two were standing in front of a large white motor home, and they were smiling at the camera.

"Who's the guy?" Frank asked.

"I don't know," Joe said, "but they look as if they're having a good time. Maybe we should add his name to our list of people to talk to."

"Yeah, once we know who he is," Frank replied. "We can't just take the picture and show it to people. We'll have to keep our eyes open and hope we run into him. Meanwhile, I think we've covered everything here."

Frank and Joe stepped out of the trailer and locked up. They were passing a small red- and black-striped tent with yellow question marks floating in the design, when a man standing in front of it barked, "Step right up."

Frank and Joe glanced behind them to be sure he was talking to them. The man grinned and beckoned them to come closer.

Of medium height, the man had a pencil-thin mustache. He wore tuxedo pants with shiny black piping up the sides, and a T-shirt. On a small table sat three pitchers of clear liquid. Across the side of the trailer were the words Marlin Randolf—Magician, Illusionist, Prestidigitator.

He held a wand in his hand, and as Frank and Joe paused, he tapped the edge of the first pitcher. The liquid turned deep red.

"Hey," Frank said, impressed.

The magician bowed and tapped the second pitcher. The contents of the pitcher turned milky white.

Frank and Joe smiled as the performer bowed

deeply and tapped the third pitcher. As they watched, the liquid darkened and turned emerald green.

"Nice," Frank said, and Joe grinned. But the magician frowned.

"No, that's not right. It's supposed to be blue now—red, white, and blue. Get it?" He reached into his pocket and took out a tiny capsule, which he flicked into the pitcher, causing the liquid to boil. As the bubbles reached the surface, they popped, releasing thick green smoke that in seconds rose above the mouth of the pitcher and cascaded across the tabletop.

Moments later the table was entirely obscured by a thick cloud. The magician calmly reached into the cloud, extracted the pitcher, and flung its contents to the ground beside the tent. "Back to my chemistry kit, I guess."

"You mean you don't use real magic?" Joe asked, smiling.

"Sorry to disappoint you," the man said with a wink, "but it's all done with chemicals. Now, if I can figure out the right mix I should be able to make that green into blue." He stuck out his hand. "Marlin Randolf," he said. "Magician, illusionist, and prestidigitator—just like the sign says."

The Hardys shook Marlin Randolf's hand.

"You must be new," Randolf said. "I don't recognize either one of you."

"We joined yesterday," Joe said.

"Well, I'm sure you'll like circus life. We travel only during the summer, and like most traveling circuses, we're based in Sarasota, Florida, through the winter. It's too cold to travel then. You can't really heat a tent the size of the big top, and anyway, the animals would get cold. So we spend winters down south. The elephants and tigers stay healthy, and we get a nice block of time to rehearse."

"Practice makes perfect," Frank said. "By the way, did you hear about what happened to that clown, Freddie Felix, during rehearsal yesterday?"

"Oh, sure. When something like that happens word spreads like wildfire," the magician replied. "I don't know much about the clown business and I didn't really know Freddie at all, but he seemed a nice enough kid. A real shame. I don't understand why he was up there."

"I know what you mean," Joe said, nodding. "You couldn't pay me enough to go up there."

"No, I mean I don't understand why he was up there instead of Bobo," the magician said. "It was his act."

"Bobo?" Frank asked.

"Bobo Rosyberk—the clown who normally does that routine."

Frank and Joe exchanged a look.

"Well," Frank said, turning to Joe, "we'd better get back before somebody notices we're not working. Nice to meet you, Marlin."

"Okay, fellas. Welcome aboard," the magician replied.

As Frank and Joe made their way back, Frank said, "That was an interesting piece of information. I wonder why Freddie went up instead of Bobo?"

"Sounds as if we should talk to Bobo Rosyberk," Joe said.

But Frank and Joe had chores to do first. They rolled the heavy steel elephant pedestals in under the big top. Then they unloaded hundred-pound coils of electrical cable from the trucks and carried in huge spotlights.

Though their coworkers remained as untalkative as they had been at breakfast, the Hardys managed to get a description of Bobo's trailer. Between chores, they headed to the spot where it was parked.

The trailer was easy to identify. Parked slightly apart from the rest, it was the biggest of them all—the size of a city bus. From a distance it looked beautiful. Its extravagant paint job showed a huge, colorful clown and bright, cartoon-style lettering that said Bobo's Here!

As Frank and Joe got closer, they could see the trailer was actually pretty run down. It needed a new coat of paint, and its silver trim was corroded and tarnished, with several pieces hanging loose.

Frank knocked at the torn screen door. After a moment a man's voice called, "Just a minute."

They waited thirty seconds . . . sixty . . . then a minute and a half.

"I wonder what's taking so long," Frank said. "This trailer's not *that* big."

"I'm not looking in any more windows," Joe said.

Just then the doorknob clicked.

"I guess you won't have to," Frank said, stepping slightly back. He was about to speak, but then froze. So did Joe.

In the doorway stood the big, cigar-smoking clown they'd seen the day before. He still wore a yellow polka-dotted jacket and baggy red plaid pants. His green hair still stuck out above his ears, and his face was still bright with whiteface. But his expression looked strange. Beneath his glittering eyes, he wore a twisted grin.

Suddenly his hand came up fast from behind his back. Frank and Joe saw a flash of silver as a large, nickel-plated revolver appeared in the clown's white-gloved hand. The gun's muzzle pointed straight at Joe's heart, and before either brother could move, the clown's finger squeezed the trigger.

5

JOE KNEW THERE WAS no way the shooter could miss at this range. But no explosion sounded. Joe just heard a loud snap. Something poked Joe's chest. He looked down to see a plastic rod sticking from the gun's muzzle. A red flag hung from it. Bang! You're Dead! it said.

The clown chuckled. "Another one bites the dust," he said. He turned and began to reload the prop, stuffing the flag back down the gun barrel.

Joe's heart was racing a mile a minute. His fists were clenched. Frank, sensing his brother was about to smash the clown in his big red nose, quickly stepped between the two.

"Are you Bobo Rosyberk?" Frank asked.

The clown nodded as he turned away. "That's

me, in the flesh." He went back into his trailer, leaving the door open. Frank turned to his brother as if to ask if this was enough of an invitation to follow. Joe shrugged, and the brothers went in.

The trailer looked as if a tornado had just passed through it. Clothes, bottles, and cans littered the floor. Ashtrays filled with cigar butts cluttered every visible surface, even the top of the small TV that sat on the coffee table.

The windows were grimy and looked to Frank as if they had never been opened. He noticed old newspaper clippings taped to the wall and realized they pictured a younger, happier-looking Rosyberk.

"Sorry about the mess. You'd think my wife could find a few minutes to clean this place," the clown said, shuffling over to a beat-up recliner. He fell into it so heavily that a dust cloud rose. "But no. She's too busy rehearsing, so this place stays a dump."

Rosyberk appeared to be in his late fifties, with a big stomach, puffy face, and bloodshot eyes. "As if I didn't get her the job in the first place," he added, speaking to no one in particular.

He grabbed a fistful of tiny pretzels from a bowl. Stuffing them into his mouth, he said, "Every time I get riled up, I have to eat." Crumbs fell from his mouth. "So, what are you boys here for, anyway?"

"Well, we're new to the show," Frank said,

"and we wanted to introduce ourselves, get to meet people."

Bobo frowned as he reached for his cigar and, puffing deeply, let out a cloud of blue-gray smoke. Squinting at their coveralls, he said, "New roustabouts, eh? You guys usually come and go so fast nobody gets a chance to meet you—and I never saw any come introduce themselves."

Bobo peered at the Hardys a moment, sucking his cigar. "You boys want something to drink?" he asked. "Help yourselves. There's sodas in the fridge."

"That's okay," Frank said. "Thanks anyway."

"You've got a great collection of clips," Joe said, nodding at the wall.

Rosyberk grunted. "Thirty years ago I was the most famous clown working. Everyone knew who Bobo Rosyberk was." He shook his head, scowling, and took another puff of his cigar. "But you get older, put on a few pounds. Suddenly the pratfalls aren't so easy—and certainly not the high wire. New clowns are always trying to crowd you out. For veterans like me it means our days are numbered." He crammed another handful of pretzels into his mouth but didn't let his chewing interrupt his speech.

"No one's got respect for older clowns these days. You know there's only seventy thousand or so clowns in the whole world? In Russia they got it right, though. Clowns there are looked up to like orchestra conductors or concert pianists. To join the Moscow State Circus you have to study at the Moscow State College of Circus and Variety Arts for *seven years*. They know clowning's an art, and they give it its proper respect. Maybe I oughta just leave and go to Russia."

"You mentioned the high wire," Frank said, gently steering the clown back on track. "We saw Freddie Felix fall off the wire yesterday. It was a pretty bad fall."

Rosyberk snorted. "He was one of those young ones I'm talking about."

"We heard he was doing the act you usually do. Is that what you mean by being squeezed out?" Joe asked.

Bobo took a long swallow from a can of soda. "Na-a-ah. I asked him to fill in for me."

"Oh, really?" Frank said, trying to seem casual.

"Yeah. I stepped in a pothole on my way to rehearsal and hurt my ankle." He held up his foot, showing a dingy gray bandage wrapped around the ankle.

Joe wondered how the bandage could have gotten so dirty in just one day. "Did you go to a doctor?" he asked.

"No. It's just a little sprain. I wrapped it myself. Doc Greene—she'd just nag me some more about losing weight and cleaning up my act. I wasn't in the mood to hear it. Anyway, it's a lot better today. I just didn't want to go on the wire with it, so I asked Freddie to sub for me. He's

47

got his eye on a full-time job, so I knew he'd say yes."

Suddenly Bobo lurched out of the chair to his feet. "It's still not perfect. See?" He began limping around, grimacing.

"It doesn't look too swollen," Joe remarked.

"Not now, but you should've seen it yesterday," the clown said.

Frank and Joe exchanged a look. They were thinking the same thing. Bobo was faking his injury. Maybe the old clown was the one trying to eliminate a rival.

Just then the door opened and a woman's voice filled the room. "Are you still loafing around on your big fat—"

The Hardys turned and the voice abruptly stopped as a young woman appeared. She had long black hair, and she was wearing jeans and a T-shirt. She seemed startled to see the visitors.

"If it isn't my darling wife," Bobo said, his voice dripping with sarcasm. "Dearest, meet Frank and Joe Hardy, the new roustabouts. My wife, Celina Stiletto."

"Roustabouts?" Celina said. "Bobo, that one went down with the *Titanic*. They're *workers*. When are you gonna join the twentieth century?"

"When you start cleaning this trailer," Bobo said. "It's a pigsty."

"If you want a maid, go hire one," Celina snapped. "Not that we have the money. Anyway, I'm just here for my case." She began tossing clothes aside, hunting for something. "I've got practice with Marlin Randolf this afternoon. At least *someone* in this family does a little extra work instead of sitting around all day."

She flung things to the floor. "I can never find anything in this dump. Oh, here it is," she said, uncovering a rectangular aluminum case similar to the kind photographers use. Flicking the snaps and opening the lid, she glanced down at a dozen shining knives nestled in purple-velvet-lined compartments, then snapped the case shut.

"We were just talking about Freddie Felix falling yesterday," Frank said. "These boys knew Freddie."

"Oh, yeah. What a shame," Celina said. "He was a nice kid, too. What happened? Did he slip?"

"Shows how much you know," Bobo said. "Nah, he took the wrong pin up. A real one instead of the breakaway."

"That's just so typical of this show," Celina said. "If somebody *can* mess up, they will. How's Dan taking it?"

"Dan?" Joe asked.

"Behemoth Dan, the strong man," Celina said. "He and Freddie are buddies."

"Gossip, gossip, gossip," Bobo said. "Is there anybody's business you *don't* get into?"

"I know what's going on because I go outside this trailer once in a while instead of sitting around stuffing my face and watching a busted TV."

"Well," Frank said, not wanting to get caught in the middle of a domestic dispute, "we'd better get back to work."

"Right," Joe quickly echoed.

When Frank and Joe were alone outside, Joe said, "Bobo's pretty bad tempered for a clown."

"It's been a long time since he was the guy in those clippings," Frank said. "And I doubt if all the eating and smoking have exactly helped his career. No wonder he's worried about the younger clowns crowding him out."

"Do you think he faked that twisted ankle of his?" Joe said.

"It would be easy enough to do," Frank said. "It's the perfect excuse. All he had to do was wrap a bandage around it and limp. He didn't even show it to the doctor, so there's no one to confirm it. And now it's practically impossible to disprove."

"So maybe Bobo's the one trying to eliminate a rival," Joe said.

"What if Tiny and Bobo were working together to get rid of a threat to them both?"

"Let's go meet Behemoth Dan," Joe said. "If he and Freddie were friends, he might know something."

Frank and Joe got directions to the strong man's trailer. They went over to it and knocked, but Behemoth Dan wasn't around. They decided to swing by again later. As they were walking away, Frank said, "Don't look now, Joe, but here comes the big boss."

Sure enough, Mickey Barnes was heading straight for them. "Where have you guys been? Gus has been looking for you. Look, one of you go help unload the Flying Falbos' truck. The other head on over to the cat cages—they're under the blue- and white-striped tent out behind the big top. Jim Buck's gonna clean them out later, and he'll need three or four bales of fresh hay for kitty litter. You'll find the bales outside the tent, where the hay wagon drops them off. Just set them inside near the cages for Jim. Did I just see you coming from Behemoth Dan's trailer?"

"We figured we'd introduce ourselves," Frank said quickly. "We didn't see him there, though."

"Dan won't be back until this afternoon. I guess you heard he had a sick aunt to check on. Don't worry about Dan, though," the show boss said. "Just look out for yourselves. There's lots of work to get done. After you're done with what I told you, check with Gus to see what else he's got for you," he called over his shoulder as he hurried off.

Frank and Joe split up. Joe headed for the Flying Falbos Aerial Act's truck, and Frank went to take care of the tigers.

Frank found the cat tent easily. It was a small blue-and-white one, open in front and back. On the ground outside the entrance sat six bales of hay in a loose cluster. They had obviously been shoved off the back of a wagon. Frank grabbed the first, wriggling his fingers under the tight metal binding wire, and headed in under the tent.

Beneath the tent's peaked top were six bright red wheeled cages, three on each side, one tiger to each cage. The tent smelled strongly of the animals and of the hay in their cages. All six huge, striped beasts stared as Frank came in.

One especially large cat, which had been noisily lapping water from a bowl the size of a kitchen sink, raised its eyes just enough to watch Frank. Frank dropped the bale of hay beside its cage and paused to rub his hands. He was not wearing work gloves, and the wires that bound the fifty-pound bales cut into his fingers. He spotted a pair of heavy canvas gloves on top of an empty cage. Slipping them on, he went out for the next bale.

On his third trip he was surprised to notice what looked like a high-powered rifle leaning against the wall. Looking at it more closely, he recognized the extra-wide-bored barrel of a tranquilizer gun.

Frank dropped the fourth bale beside a cage. Most of the tigers seemed to take him for granted, as if all humans were alike to them. They sat blinking at him like very large, tame housecats. Only the tiger that had stopped lapping water—its head as wide as Frank's chest—continued to stare at him intently.

When Frank came back and dropped the sixth and final bale, he paused to wipe his sweaty forehead. A movement off to his left caught his eye. Turning, Frank froze.

Stepping out its open cage door no more than twenty feet away was the huge tiger that had been eyeing him.

As it dropped smoothly to the ground, the big cat spotted Frank. Its ears cocked forward, and its eyes locked on Frank's. It began inching slowly toward him, the way a cat stalks a mouse.

Frank knew he didn't have a prayer of outrunning or even dodging the huge predator, which was now padding across the dirt toward him.

Suddenly the animal stopped. Still staring at Frank, it went into a crouch, its hindquarters bunched up and its thick tail flicking and twitching. Then it charged, accelerating to full speed like a racing car. Its head level, ears flat, bone white fangs exposed, five hundred pounds of killer cat raced straight at Frank.

Chapter
6

"CATCH!" FRANK SHOUTED. Hoping desperately to distract the tiger, Frank pulled off his gloves and flung them at the tiger. They flew past either side of its head and reflexively the cat reacted. It reached out a huge paw, suddenly playful, as if trying to snag one of the gloves. Frank turned and dove toward the tranquilizer gun, snatching it up, spinning, and, as the tiger looked up, pulling the trigger.

Pop!

At the sharp noise, the big cat whipped around. A tranquilizer dart the length of a pencil dangled from the animal's upper leg. The tiger twisted around, straining to reach the dart, but then the beast stopped and shook its massive head. It looked around at Frank again. For a moment the tiger just stood there, its paws wide and rigid as if to keep its balance. Then the yellow eyes fluttered, and the animal's breathing slowed.

The huge carnivore suddenly sat. It seemed disoriented and unable to focus. Then it stood and tried to step forward, but it faltered and sat back down on its haunches. It eased down to its stomach, then its side. Its head rested on the ground, and where its huge tongue licked its chops Frank saw white foam at its mouth.

"Frank!"

Frank turned and saw Joe racing into the tent.

"What happened?" the younger Hardy asked.

"About two more seconds and I'd have been cat food," Frank said, and let out a large sigh.

Frank and Joe cautiously approached the tiger, which was now lying on its side, its chest slowly rising and falling. The Hardys were surprised to see the animal's huge, glazed eyes still half open.

"How long you think he'll be out?" Joe asked.

"I don't know what the dosage is, but since the gun was here, it must be for cats. We'd better find Jim Buck, though."

After asking around, Frank and Joe found the trainer at the chow tent. At first the cat tamer didn't believe the Hardys.

"Out of its cage?" he said. "Impossible." But when Frank and Joe finally convinced him, he ran all the way back with them from the other side of the lot.

With the help of some other workers they wheeled the empty cage close to the five-hundred-pound feline, then dragged it gently back into its enclosure.

"Wait a second," Buck said as he went to lock the cage. "Where's the lock pin?"

After checking the cage and the ground around it, Buck got another piece of metal from his equipment box. When it was safely in place, he turned to Frank and Joe. "Now, how about telling me how this happened?"

"No idea," Frank said. He explained that he had been bringing in the hay when he had turned and seen the tiger free.

"That pin didn't just jump out by itself," the trainer said doubtfully. "And since you were the only one in here—"

"Hey, anyone could have slipped in here," Frank said. "I mean, with the tent open like this."

"Look, most of the time I'm with the cats," Buck said. "But I'm not exactly in a position to post a twenty-four-hour guard on them."

"Has this ever happened before?" Joe interrupted.

"Never," the cat tamer said.

"Even if the pin just came out because it wasn't in all the way," Frank said, "how could a heavy barred door just swing open by itself?"

"The cats are always rubbing against the bars,"

the cat tamer said. "If the pin wasn't in, the door could have easily swung open."

"But that still doesn't explain why the pin isn't right near the cage," Joe said. "And it also seems awfully coincidental this should happen when Frank was in here."

"I don't know what to tell you guys. Why would someone want to let one of the cats loose?" Buck asked. Then he turned and walked away.

After the others had gone, Frank and Joe stood beside the wheeled cart.

"Well?" Joe asked as he and Frank examined the cage's lock. "What do you think? An accident or not?"

"I don't know," Frank said. "But that lock pin didn't walk away by itself. Let's look around a little."

Frank and Joe searched the trodden grass until Joe stopped and looked down. "I found it," he said. He reached slightly under the cat cage and retrieved the heavy, L-shaped steel pin from the ground. Handing it to his brother, he asked, "So, what do you think? Did it come out by accident? Maybe it wasn't in all the way?"

"Could be," Frank said, though his tone revealed that he wasn't convinced. He studied the pin. "Or else someone took it out."

"You mean as a prank? A little initiation for one of the new workers?"

Frank shook his head. "We've been asking a

lot of questions, Joe. What if someone worried about the answers we're getting? That person could have followed me in here, waited until I turned my back, then seen a chance . . ."

The older Hardy didn't need to finish the sentence. He checked his watch. "Look, we have a while before it's time to unload the trapeze artists' stuff. What do you say we try Behemoth Dan's place again?"

Frank and Joe were just coming around the edge of the big top with Frank in the lead. "Wait a second, Joe," he said. "Look over there."

Joe followed his brother's gaze. A large white motor home sat parked twenty yards off, between a pair of other trailers.

"So?"

"It's the one in the snapshot in Freddie's trailer—in the background, remember?" Frank paused, then called to a worker passing with a coil of electrical cable over his shoulder.

"Hey, we're looking for Gus's trailer. It's the motor home there, right?"

The harried worker snorted and shook his head as he kept walking. "The white one? Gus should be so lucky. No, that's Willie Thurston's—the show vet. Gus's is a little green one clear across the lot." As the worker hurried off, Frank called out his thanks.

"Well, now we know who the guy in the photo is," Frank said, turning to Joe.

This time they found Behemoth Dan at home.

Working out beneath a canvas awning in front of his trailer, he looked every inch the classic circus strong man, with a barrel chest, thick arms, and a neck as wide as his shaved head. His sleeveless yellow sweatshirt had armholes so ragged he might have torn the sleeves off with his bare hands, Joe thought. His wide leather lifting belt looked like something a plowhorse would wear.

Dan was standing behind a set of barbells as Frank and Joe approached. Tallying the weights, Frank realized the strong man was about to try lifting over six hundred pounds. As Dan rubbed his palms and fingers with chalk, then squatted behind the bar and concentrated, Frank and Joe hung back, so as not to interrupt.

Keeping his back straight, Dan gripped the bar, adjusted his hold, then suddenly stood, lifting the bar across his thighs. It pulled his thick arms taut and made his huge shoulders bulge. He jerked the bar to shoulder height, then, grunting loudly, he shifted his feet and shot the bar straight overhead, locking his elbows. The ends of the bar actually sagged from the huge weight it was supporting. Dan held it several seconds, puffing loudly through his mouth, then stepped back, dropping the bar at his feet, where it thumped in the dirt.

"Nice lift," Frank said appreciatively.

The strong man looked up, his bald head shining and a small gold hoop gleaming in his left earlobe. Eyeing Frank and Joe, he asked,

"Who're you?" His deep voice was not at all friendly.

The Hardys introduced themselves. Dan nodded soberly, still not smiling.

"How'd everything turn out with your aunt?" Joe asked. "Is she all right?"

The strong man stared at the younger Hardy. "My aunt?"

"Mickey Barnes told us you were visiting her," Frank said.

"Oh," the strong man said quickly. "Yeah. She's fine. Now, what was it you came to talk to me about?"

"We were there when Freddie Felix fell yesterday," Frank said. "Someone said a real juggling pin got switched for a prop one. We're friends of Freddie's and we're trying to piece together what happened."

"I wouldn't know," the strong man said. His eyes seemed to shift uneasily away from Frank and Joe.

"We heard you and Freddie Felix are friends," Joe said. "I'm surprised you're not more concerned about him."

"You heard we're friends, huh?" Dan said, glaring. "Heard from who?"

Frank was surprised by the big man's belligerence. He decided it might be better not to mention any names.

"No one in particular. Just around."

"What else did you hear around?" Dan's mouth was set in a sneer.

"Nothing," Frank said. Then, deciding to take the offensive, he asked, "Why? Have you got any secrets people aren't supposed to talk about?"

The big man scowled. "Not at all."

"No?" Joe said.

"That's what I said," Dan replied. He reached for a bottle of Electro-Lyte workout cooler he had on a chair nearby and drained it. "Well, I'm done for now." He turned toward the door, pulled it open, and without another word went inside.

Frank turned to Joe. "So much for getting anything more out of him today. Look, we should get back to work anyway."

Frank and Joe were passing one of the concession stands when Joe said, "Hold on a second. Let me grab a chocolate bar. I'm going to starve to death trying to live on that poison they give us in the chow tent."

Frank and Joe stopped near a stand about fifty yards from Dan's trailer. Joe bought the biggest bar sold there and began unwrapping it. "This just cost me a good chunk of my week's paycheck."

"Joe, hold on. I think maybe we can get a look inside Dan's trailer."

Joe stood with his back to the strong man's home, but Frank, facing his brother, looking over his shoulder, had a perfect view. "Behemoth just

came out. Now he's locking his door . . . bingo—
he's walking away."

"Beautiful," Joe said. "Let's go." Shoving the
rest of the chocolate bar into his mouth, the
younger brother flipped the empty wrapper into
a trash can, and he and Frank walked quickly
back to the trailer.

As Frank casually stood guard, half shielding
Joe from sight, the younger Hardy got to work
on the lock. Thirty seconds later a sharp click
sounded.

"What took you so long?" Frank asked, grinning as he followed his brother up the creaky
metal ladder.

Behemoth Dan's living space was small, neat,
and relatively clean. Dan had a bed, bureau, and
full-length mirror. Several leopard-skin capes
hung on hangers beside a small back window facing the woods.

On a coffee table lay issues of body-building
magazines, their covers showing hugely muscled
men and powerful-looking women in tiny briefs,
striking poses that highlighted their enormous,
tanned, vein-mapped bodies. On a counter sat
large brown bottles labeled Vitamin C, B-complex,
Desiccated Liver, and Powdered Brewer's Yeast.

"Looks like the Behemoth's seriously into vitamins and health food," Joe observed.

"His body's his livelihood," Frank said.

Joe began rooting through the closet. He went
clear down to the bottom, searching even Dan's

shoes, when his brother said, "Hey, Joe, check this out."

The younger Hardy turned to see Frank with a shoebox-size metal box he'd drawn from under the bed. A shiny padlock hung from the front.

"What do you think?" Frank said.

Eyeing the lock, Joe said, "Shouldn't be too hard."

"Try to make it a rush job, okay?" Frank said. "We don't want Dan walking in on us."

"I second that," Joe said, taking the lock firmly in his hand as he fit a tiny ridged pick into the keyhole. He probed carefully, feeling the spring tension of its pins. A few moments later he said, "I think this should about do it."

Just then they heard a loud creak. Frank and Joe looked up suddenly. There was someone on the metal stepladder outside the door. Joe shoved the box back under the bed.

Looking around desperately, Frank and Joe realized the compact trailer offered no place to hide.

Then the unmistakable sound of keys jangled at the lock.

Chapter

7

FRANK WHIRLED TOWARD the counter. He took a half step and snatched up a large brown bottle, unscrewed the lid, upended the glass over his cupped palm, and poured out a handful of coarse white sea salt. Drawing back his fist, Frank waited until the door opened. Then, the instant Behemoth Dan came through it, Frank flung the salt into his eyes.

"Hey!" Dan shouted as he doubled over and shook his head. His hands shot reflexively to his face, and he pressed the heels of his palms to his eyes. Then he made another sound—of rage. He spread his arms wide, and though his eyes stayed tightly shut, he charged farther into the tiny trailer and plowed right into Joe.

As they crashed against the wall, the big man wrapped his arms around Joe's waist. Dan's biceps bulged as he squeezed, determined to crush Joe. Joe shoved his hands beneath the big man's jaw to force his head back, but Dan fought back. He had a death grip on the younger Hardy, whose face turned bright red. Frank grabbed Dan's wrist in a martial arts hold and dug his thumb into a pressure point below the thumb. Dan resisted, but then, with a furious shout, let go.

Dan still stood between Joe and the door, so Joe stepped in and wrapped an arm around the big man's waist. The younger Hardy pivoted left, put all his weight behind the move, and threw Dan aside, sending him crashing against the wall. The sound was enormous, and the small trailer rocked.

Frank and Joe dove through the open door. Glad that no one was near or was looking their way, they darted around the edge of the trailer toward the woods behind.

"Close one," Joe whispered, struggling to catch his breath as they found refuge in the thick foliage. Then they heard the trailer's door bounce loudly against the outside wall. The next moment a loud crash of snapping twigs and branches told them Dan was charging into the woods after them.

"It's not over yet," Frank said.

Frank and Joe bolted and soon were racing at

full tilt, dodging trees and hurdling ferns as thin branches whipped their faces. Behind them, Dan sounded like a runaway locomotive crashing through the undergrowth. Frank and Joe realized he wasn't wasting time dodging but was simply plowing ahead with brute strength.

"He's gaining on us," Joe panted.

Frank stopped short. Looking up, he saw the trees' thick, leafy cover just ten or twelve feet overhead.

"Come on," he said. *"Quick."* Wiping his palms on his pants legs, he crouched, then leaped to a branch overhead. In an instant he had hoisted himself among the thick branches. Joe followed, his sneakers squeaking against the rough bark.

Moments later Frank and Joe sat panting among the leaves twenty feet above the forest floor. A commotion sounded below, and they spotted Behemoth Dan's pale, shining head as he came charging through the foliage.

Swiping at branches, the strong man raced right past their tree and went another five yards. Then he stopped. Pausing, he listened. Frank and Joe saw him spin in one direction, then another. He listened again. After a moment he angrily swatted a fern, flung a handful of leaves to the ground, and stalked back the way he had come.

Later that afternoon Joe climbed the semi's ladder, hoping to flop into his bunk for a quick catnap. He had had so little sleep the night before that after hours of carrying, hauling, lifting, and dragging, and then the footrace with Dan, he was ready for some rest. He was glad to find the truck empty, but as he approached his bunk, he saw something on his blanket—a folded sheet of white paper with his name on it.

He opened it.

Joe, if you want to know why my father dislikes Freddie Felix, meet me behind the elephant trailer after tonight's show.

                                        Shahela

"What do you think?" Joe asked his brother after Frank had read the note. It was late afternoon, and Frank and Joe were walking to the chow tent for dinner. They were hungry, but they already knew better than to expect a good meal. Overcooked spaghetti with watered-down sauce, undercooked gray burgers, or, worst of all, the dreaded veal marengo weren't exactly mouth-watering prospects.

"Any guesses what it's all about?" Joe continued, taking the note back from his brother. He folded it, then slipped it into his pocket.

"Whatever Darbar's reason for hating Freddie, it would have to be pretty strong for him to risk killing him," Frank said. "Definitely go hear what Shahela has to say. Just don't take too long.

"In the meantime, let's use the time we have now before setup for tonight's show. If Freddie and the vet are as tight as it seemed in that snapshot, the vet might know something. Let's swing by his trailer."

The show vet's trailer appeared exactly as in the photo: a tall, white motor home.

"These things are expensive," Frank said as he knocked beside the door, on the metal wall. "I'll bet this ate a big chunk of his salary."

A moment later the door opened, though barely enough for a face to appear. "Yes?" said a short, thin-faced man wearing glasses, who appeared to be in his forties. It was definitely the person in Freddie's photo.

"Are you Dr. Thurston?" Frank asked.

"That's right. What can I do for you?"

"Well," Frank said, "my brother and I are new workers—I'm Frank and this is Joe"—Frank stepped aside and Joe nodded—"and this afternoon I had to shoot one of the tigers with a tranquilizer dart. We're wondering if there might be any aftereffects Jim Buck should know about."

"But why would you have to tranquilize one of the tigers in the first place?" the vet asked.

Joe leaned around his brother. "Why don't you invite us in for a minute and we'll tell you all about it."

The vet hesitated, then nodded. "Okay, but just be careful not to open the door too wide." As Thurston backed inside, Frank turned to shoot Joe a quizzical look. Joe shrugged and gave his brother a slight shove.

As Frank and Joe slipped inside, they beheld an amazing spectacle. The room was literally a nest of activity. At least two dozen uncaged birds filled the trailer. Small green ones, blue ones, slightly larger yellow ones, and yellow- and black-striped ones perched on the table, counters, backs of chairs, and curtain rods—in short, everywhere, singing, chirping, ruffling their feathers, and fluttering about.

"It's a regular aviary!" Frank exclaimed.

Thurston smiled. "I confess I'm an amateur ornithologist and an avid bird lover. Now you see why I'm careful about the door. I don't want any of my beauties flying out."

"Uh-huh," Frank said. "What kinds are they, exactly?"

"The small green-and-blue ones are finches, and the larger yellow or yellow-striped ones are canaries—my two favorites," the vet said. "The canaries sing and the finches chirp."

Thurston went on to say that, among birds, the males generally had more colorful plumage than the females, to attract them. He also told them that in a forest, birds chirped to warn other birds of where their territory was, and that both finches and canaries were seed birds, meaning they ate seeds only and never nuts or fruit. He explained that that was why they had straight, not hooked, beaks.

As Thurston spoke, the whole room seemed alive, with birds hopping, tilting their heads, chirping, and flying at any given moment, fluttering from place to place. Most, though, seemed to stay on a large branch imbedded in a tub of sand, where their droppings fell without making too much mess.

"How do they know to return to the branch before they, uh, do their business?" Joe asked.

"They don't," Thurston answered. "But the branch is their home base, and they return to it often enough that cleanup in here doesn't usually get too out of hand."

Joe noticed the finches had very smooth-looking, almost shiny bodies. One had a scarlet mask, with an iridescent green back and a yellow belly. The canaries were more fully yellow, although they had brownish gray stripes on their backs.

"I see you admiring their colors. Am I right?" Thurston asked. "Let me introduce you to one of my favorites."

The small, thin man offered a crooked finger to a canary perched on the lampshade of a large, glass-based table lamp. "Shelley, say hello to our guests," Thurston said. The bird stepped onto the veterinarian's finger, its tiny feet grasping it below the knuckle. The bird tilted its head one way, then the other, as if studying each brother in turn.

"Shelley's a tiger canary," the vet said. "Normally they're not this friendly, but I spend a lot of time socializing my birds. Would you believe his best friend's a finch named Pete?" The doctor turned to look for Pete, but after a moment seemed to catch himself. "I could talk about my birds all day, but why don't you tell me about this afternoon. What exactly happened with the tiger?"

After Frank recounted the incident, glossing over the mysteriously removed cage pin, the wide-eyed vet shook his head.

"It's lucky you're such a good marksman," he said. "You could easily have been mauled or even killed. As to aftereffects for the tiger, I wouldn't worry. The dose in that tranquilizer is strong to make it act fast, but those cats are big. Their bodies can handle it."

"Seems as if there've been a few accidents lately," Frank said. "I guess you heard what happened to Freddie Felix yesterday. Do you know him well?"

"We're friends, yes."

"That was pretty surprising, wouldn't you say, given his reputation for being really careful?"

Joe was browsing idly around, glancing at the books on Thurston's shelves. The vet looked over his shoulder at him.

"Yes," Thurston said. "Well, I suppose that's true."

"No ideas how it might have happened, then?" Frank persisted. "Freddie confusing pins like that?"

"Well, with so much going on here, you know,

71

it's easy to get, uh, distracted and . . . overlook something."

Frank couldn't help noticing how often the vet turned to look at Joe. Did he think the younger Hardy was going to slip one of Thurston's pets into his pocket?

"Hey," Joe said, "what's all this?"

Frank turned. The vet was already looking behind him, and now he shot to his feet.

Joe stood beside a shelf with an infrared bulb, like the kind used to keep restaurant food warm, shining down on two small white eggs nestled in a bed of straw.

"Oh, just my breeding area," Thurston said.

"You keep them warm under heat lamps, huh?" Joe asked. "Makes sense."

"Yes—to strictly regulate them, of course. And I turn them four times a day so they heat evenly."

"When will they hatch?" Joe asked.

"Oh, pretty soon," said the vet.

"Man, I'd love to be here to see that. Check these out, Frank."

Frank turned to join Joe.

Looking down at the two eggs, which were just a fraction the size of chicken eggs, Frank noticed they were slightly off-white. He was about to ask about this when there was a deafening crash of shattering glass, and the trailer was suddenly plunged into darkness. The Hardys spun around and immediately sensed an explosion of activity as the air came alive with dozens of beating wings. The tiny trailer filled with squawking and screeching, the birds filling the air with a thick and deafening cloud of sharp claws and pointed beaks.

Chapter

8

"CALM THESE BIRDS DOWN!" Frank said as he shielded his face from the swirling cloud of beaks and claws pricking his arms, head, and neck. Amid the sound of panicked tweets and shrill squawks he felt the small, feathered bodies buffet his shoulders.

Through the noise Frank heard Willie Thurston calling, "Easy, easy," and glimpsed the vet desperately yanking out bureau drawers, hunting for something as he, too, tried to shield his eyes. Then a flashlight beam cut the darkness, creating a surreal tableau as the shadows of the frantic birds swooped and fluttered across the walls and ceiling.

"I have an electric lantern here somewhere,"

Thurston called, his flashlight in hand. A few moments later a flickering white camper lantern lit. The birds seemed immediately to calm down somewhat.

"What happened?" Joe asked.

Thurston shook his head. "I feel so stupid." He gestured toward a pile of glass shards on the floor. He continued to try to soothe his pets. "I accidentally knocked over the lamp. Of course the sudden noise panicked them. I'm sorry, but I need to clean up this glass and it'll be easier to calm them without strangers here. Would you please excuse me?"

"No problem," Frank said. "Come on, Joe. We'll come back another time."

Leaving the trailer, Frank and Joe headed back toward the semi.

"So?" Frank asked. "What do you think? The vet's kind of a strange guy, isn't he?"

"Sure is," Joe said, glancing back at the trailer, where bird silhouettes still fluttered behind the curtains. "How could he live with all those birds? Disgusting."

"I can't figure out who's more nervous, he or his little pets," Frank said. "Maybe he'll calm down later and we can get some info on Freddie out of him."

The show that night went without a hitch. Frank and Joe carried in the fire-eater's flaming torches, rolled the heavy steel elephant pedestals into the ring, and Joe wheeled out the chimp act's tall, shining unicycle. During Queen Sasha's equestrian performance, Frank ran under the lights to straighten a wooden curb that one of the performing horses had kicked.

As the crowd finally filed out and the cleanup crew and tent riggers trudged in, Joe said to Frank, "Wouldn't you know it. That stupid chimp spat at me. Mean-spirited little thing. Anyway, I'm gonna clean up, then I'm off to meet Shahela."

"Catch you later, then," Frank said. "Just don't be long. Gus and Barnes'll wonder where you are."

In the semidarkness behind the elephant trailer, Joe watched the huge shapes ponderously shift position through the trailer's slatted sides. Occasionally a curious trunk curled out from between the slats, puffing loudly as it explored the ground for peanuts and raising tiny puffs of dirt. Then a slim figure in a long pale dress stepped around the corner of the trailer.

"Joe?" she asked.

"Over here, Shahela," Joe said.

"I am glad you came," the young woman said, approaching. "I left the note because I thought you deserved to know more about why my father hates Freddie. I felt I owed you some explanation after you tried to protect me this afternoon."

"You mean when I saved you from your own pet?" Joe said, a bit embarrassed.

"But you did not know Rosmali was my pet, so what you did was brave." She shook her head. "I feel so bad that Freddie got hurt. My father does not, though. You see, Freddie was talking to me and showing me attention, and then a few days ago he invited me out for coffee."

"Invited you for coffee?" Joe said. "What's the big deal?"

"To my father it *is* a big deal. He's very traditional, and for a young man to ask me out, or even to talk to me without my father present, is much too forward. My father thought it was an improper advance. It's a cultural difference. Back in India something like this would never be allowed. And also Freddie is just a clown. My father believes he is beneath us and has no business talking to me."

"Is this why you wanted to meet me so secretly, so your father wouldn't think *I* was making improper advances and being too forward, also? After all, I'm even lower than a clown. I'm just a worker."

Joe saw Shahela smile in the darkness. "To be truthful, yes. If he knew we were meeting like this now, he would become furious. I hate that he's so old-fashioned. I want to live like an American girl—free, not a slave to all my father's old ways."

"Shahela, you know your father better than anyone," Joe said. "Do you think he'd try to hurt Freddie to keep him from pursuing you?"

Shahela paused thoughtfully. "To be truthful, I don't know. Family is so very important to him, I don't know how far my father might go." She paused and looked into Joe's eyes. "I just don't know."

Later that night Frank and Joe sat on Frank's bunk. Frank leaned against the splintery wood divider separating his compartment from the one behind, while Joe propped himself back on his elbows, his legs dangling above his own bunk.

Except for a faint, flickering yellow light coming from the front of the semi, where a worker had set a candle in a dish on the floor beside his bunk, the truck was dark. The candle was an obvious fire hazard, but there were so many hazards that the Hardys knew that complaining would be pointless and would probably just win them enemies.

As the semi barreled along the highway, Joe's legs gently swaying with its motion, Frank and Joe spoke in quiet tones barely louder than the hum of the road.

"Well, if Darbar dislikes Freddie as much as it sounds," Frank said, after hearing about Joe's meeting with Shahela, "I'd say the snake charmer's a suspect, too."

Joe sighed. "Frank, we're two days into this and we still don't even know if the prop switch was deliberate. I'm still not sold that Freddie's fall wasn't just an accident. People do make mistakes, and so far we haven't found one piece of hard evidence to prove this wasn't a mix-up. I vote we drop this whole thing and catch a bus home."

"Joe, we haven't even given this a fair shot yet."

"But we're getting nowhere."

"Come on, just a little longer. Look, you're just tired. Don't decide now. Sleep on it and let me know in the morning."

Joe sighed as he slipped off the edge of the bunk to land on his bare feet. "Sleep on it," he muttered. "More like toss and turn on it. No way I'm going to get any sleep on this rolling reject from a trucker's nightmare."

The next morning, after Frank and Joe had spent two hours unloading trucks, and after they'd eaten a breakfast of burnt toast and slimy fried eggs afloat in grease, they rose from the long table and Joe said, "Okay, I've thought about it."

The younger Hardy slipped his tin plate into the huge galvanized metal washtub where dishes soaked in tepid gray water. "And I still say let's pack it in." Joe winced as he rubbed the back of his neck, stiff from another night's poor sleep. "Not only is the work hard, but the hours are long, the sleeping arrangements are terrible, and the food's putrid. Actually, I think I've finally figured out why every meal's so super spicy. It's the cook's way of disguising old ingredients."

"Joe, hang in just a little longer," Frank said. "Last night after we talked I got to thinking. When we were poking around Freddie's trailer, what's the one thing we didn't find that we should have?"

"Bus tickets out of here?"

"The breakaway pin. If the swap really was accidental, the breakaway should have still been there—and someplace pretty obvious. So why didn't it turn up?"

Joe shrugged.

"Joe, I'm going to see if I can find it."

"Be my guest," Joe said. "I'm going to hunt for some edible food. There's got to be something around here that sustains life."

After Frank and Joe split up, Frank decided to begin with a more diligent search of Freddie's trailer. When Frank and Joe had looked through it the day before, they hadn't been hunting specifically for the pin; they could have overlooked it.

Frank returned to the tiny living space and searched everywhere. He looked in the closet, under the bed, at the backs of drawers—anywhere a juggling pin might fit. In the prop carton he again saw the rubber balls and rings. This time he noted that there were several pins. But none was a breakaway.

He continued to search until he was sure that

the pin wasn't there. Where could it have gone? he wondered. And if Freddie had really simply grabbed the wrong pin, who would remove the breakaway from his trailer and why?

Frank tried to remember the setup at the high wire. If someone had switched pins just before the act, mightn't they have left the breakaway somewhere nearby? It would be a lot safer than to risk being seen carrying the prop pin away.

He decided to check the truck that held the high-wire rigging. Although the truck wasn't formally off-limits, Frank had no legitimate reason to be poking around inside, so after he'd walked to the truck and climbed aboard, he drew the door closed behind him. He would have to be quiet.

In the soft light of the truck's opaque plastic roof, Frank saw a rolled-up safety net and coils of steel cable. Winches, heavy hooks, steel rings and snaps, and heavy fasteners hung from the walls. Several coils of half-inch-thick, shiny steel cable hung from wall hooks. Two eight-foot aluminum tubular balance poles like the one Freddie had used were attached horizontally along the wall.

Frank began to search thoroughly, checking every corner. The pin would be about sixteen inches tall by six inches wide at its broadest part.

At one point Frank leaned forward to look behind the balance poles, and his head bumped a heavy swivel, which slipped off its nail. He grabbed for it, but it was too late. The piece of hardware bounced off the topmost metal tube with a loud thunk. Frank froze, waiting to see if anyone passing outside had heard and was going to check out the sound.

After a few moments, he relaxed. No one. Good. He returned the swivel to its nail, and disappointed not to have found anything, he turned toward the door. Then he paused and looked back at the tube. The sound had been a dull thunk, not the clang or bong or any similar ringing sound that he might have expected from a hollow metal tube.

Frank rapped the tube with his knuckle. Again he heard the thunk. He tried the other tube. This time he heard a bong—a metallic sound similar to what he heard when Freddie dropped the balance pole moments before falling.

Frank bent to examine the first tube. He peered into one end and was surprised he couldn't see light at the other. He stuck his hand inside. Stretching, he felt his fingertips graze something smooth, round, and hard. It was wedged in firmly, but when he pressed his neck tightly against the cold metal rim, he managed to grab it. He pulled hard and it came loose—or part of it did. Actually, it broke apart in his hand. Suspecting what it might be, Frank removed the piece and stared at it.

White with a red zigzag pattern, it was unmistakably the top of a juggling pin. No doubt the missing breakaway pin Freddie had intended to use. If the young clown had carelessly grabbed the wrong pin from his trailer, how could this one, the actual breakaway, have wound up here accidentally?

There was no way. Someone had to have jammed it in here.

And that someone was also the one who tried to kill Freddie the clown.

Suddenly Frank heard a loud squeaking of hinges.

The door began to open.

Chapter

9

FRANK SHOVED THE PIN FRAGMENT inside his coveralls and turned. The door swung open, and a shadowy silhouette peered in. "Who's there? Frank?"

It was Gus. "I thought I heard noises. What're you doing in here?"

Frank raised his hand, ran it slowly through his hair, and pretended to yawn. "Just catching a little catnap," he said, moving toward the door. "This was the quietest place I could find. It's not a problem, is it?"

"As long as you're where you need to be when there's work, I don't care. Lots of guys sack out in strange places. You're not the first. It's okay— just don't be scarce when there's carrying to do."

"Not me," Frank said, passing the foreman.

He rushed back to the trailer to find his brother.

"Joe, take a look at this," Frank said.

As Joe examined the pin fragment, Frank described how and where he had found it.

"Well, I guess you were right," Joe said, turning the piece in his hand. "Whoever swapped the pins must've worried that after Freddie fell, someone might remember seeing the pin-switcher carrying it away. So they just hid it in the nearest place handy. This definitely puts a new spin on things," Joe admitted. "Now that we know the swap was deliberate, I'm all for sticking with this until we find out who's behind it. Let's go over our list of suspects and motives."

"First," Frank began, "there's Tiny Winston. He and Freddie were rivals for a full-time job, so Winston might have wanted to squeeze Freddie out of the picture."

"And Bobo Rosyberk, who's older and near retiring, said the younger clowns were squeezing *him* out, so he could have seen Freddie as a threat to his job. Actually, with Freddie a threat to both Tiny *and* Bobo, maybe they were working together to get rid of him."

"Could be," Frank said. "And for that matter, Bobo's wife could even have been helping him. She'd have wanted Freddie out of the way so her husband wouldn't lose his job."

"I suppose," Joe said. "Though the way they

THE HARDY BOYS CASEFILES

bickered with each other, I'd be surprised if they could agree even on that. But, hey, let's not rule out Sinjay Darbar. There was no love lost between him and Freddie, and even Darbar's own daughter wasn't sure how far her father might go to stop Freddie's advances."

"We've got a full lineup of suspects," Frank said, "but before we close out the list, remember we still haven't accounted for Behemoth Dan's or Willie Thurston's weird behavior."

"Maybe it's time we did," Joe said. "What if we start with that mystery box Behemoth Dan keeps locked beneath his bed?"

Detouring past the big top, Frank and Joe looked in to see if the strong man was working out there, as they had learned he usually did. They spotted him there doing bench presses with an enormous amount of weight. Frank and Joe did an about-face to head for the strong man's trailer.

"By the way," Frank asked his brother as they walked. "Did you find any food?"

"If you can call it that," Joe said. "You know that guy who's the human cannonball? His wife sells sandwiches from their trailer. For what Tony's Pizza charges for a huge slice with the works, she sells you a thin slice of salami, a thinner slice of American cheese, and a piece of shriveled lettuce on soggy white bread dripping watered-down mayonnaise."

Joe shook his head in disgust. "The most pathetic thing about it is people were waiting in line to buy them."

They broke into Behemoth Dan's trailer again and Joe headed straight for the bed and reached underneath. After a moment of feeling around, he bent down to peer underneath.

"What's the matter?" Frank asked.

Joe straightened up. "It's gone. He probably got scared and hid it."

Frank stepped from the window and surveyed the small trailer. "That thing is too big for Dan to carry around everywhere, so it must still be in here somewhere."

Frank and Joe began to search. They looked carefully, and Joe found it under a small pile of laundry. He set the box on the bed and began to work on the lock.

"There. I think that's it."

The lock snapped, and Joe raised the box's hinged lid. Frank and Joe stared down at a dozen small brown bottles cushioned with crumpled newspaper.

"More vitamins?" Joe asked. "But why lock them up?"

Frank took out one bottle and read its label. "Joe, these aren't vitamins, they're anabolic steroids."

"Hey, this is great," Joe said. "They're illegal to own. Even if he wasn't involved with Freddie's accident, we can probably use this to squeeze some information out of him."

87

"Okay, let's go. He's probably still working out under the big top," Frank said.

Heading toward the huge striped tent, the Hardys passed performers preparing for the show, and the first "towners," as circus people called the locals, were already arriving.

"Hey," Joe said at one point as they walked. "I wonder where Willie Thurston's off to?" He nodded toward a nearby field.

Frank looked. A hundred yards across the field they saw the veterinarian crossing toward a bus stop. The nearest town was a couple of miles away. Nestled in a valley, it was a small, blue-collar factory town called Broxton. Over his shoulder, Thurston carried a loose white cloth bag.

"Laundry day, looks like," Frank said. "I guess they've got to clean their clothes sometime. There's no time to talk to Thurston now, but let's catch up with him later."

Under the big top, beside center ring, the strong man was still working out. Seated on a red vinyl lifting bench, leaning forward with his head bent, he did slow dumbbell curls, the veins of his right bicep bulging.

As Frank and Joe approached, he looked up.

"You two again," he said, sounding not at all pleased. He dropped the dumbbell in the dirt.

"We want to talk to you about that metal box you keep hidden," Frank said.

The big man shot to his feet, his face inches

from Frank's. This close, Frank could practically feel the man's power. Dan was a mountain of muscle. Though roughly Frank's height, the strong man outweighed him by a good hundred pounds—all of it muscle. The Hardys were built powerfully, but this man's shoulders looked a yard wide and supported a huge neck.

"That was you in my trailer yesterday, wasn't it?" Dan demanded, his eyes blazing.

"That's right," Frank said, eyeing the man and not backing down.

"It was both of us," Joe added, stepping in close.

"I oughtta break your necks," the strong man said, the veins in his neck bulging.

"I don't suggest you try," Joe said.

"Look, Dan," Frank said, realizing a brawl wouldn't get them anywhere, "get rough, and you'll only have more explaining to do. Anyway, if you're using steroids to bulk up, you're only hurting yourself. We want to know about Freddie Felix. Unless you start talking, we're going to tell the local police about that box."

The strong man glared at Frank and Joe.

"Start talking," Frank said. "You've got exactly five seconds before we head to Mickey Barnes's trailer and call nine one one."

"All right, wait a second," Dan said, lowering his voice and glancing around to see if anyone was nearby. "I take them, all right? I need them to be big."

"The fact that they cause cancer and all kinds of nasty side effects doesn't bother you?" Frank asked. "How does this tie in with Freddie, anyway?" he added.

The big man shrugged. "Freddie found out. He had a nosy streak, like you guys. One day he came into the trailer when I had the box open. I'm not sure he even knew what they were, but I worried he might realize later on."

"So you arranged his so-called accident to keep him quiet," Frank said.

"No way," Dan said quickly. "I wasn't even here when he fell. I was gone all day Saturday."

"To visit your aunt, or so you said," Joe added. "It's funny. When I mentioned her yesterday, it seemed as if you'd forgotten all about her."

Dan hesitated, then said, "All right, so I wasn't with my aunt. I went to New York City." Catching Frank and Joe's doubtful look, he went on, "I had a meeting with Rad Cliffson."

"Rad Cliffson, the actor?" Joe asked. The superstar's fast-paced action movies included nonstop explosions, martial arts, and Cliffson showing off his physique.

Dan nodded. "A few months ago I heard Cliffson was looking for a personal trainer. It sounded like a great job so I wrote to him. His manager sent me a letter, and we set up a time to meet at his office in New York on Saturday. That's where I was when Freddie got hurt."

"Do you still have Cliffson's letter?" Frank asked.

"I'm sure I do," Dan said.

"Then you won't mind showing it to us, will you?"

"Of course not." Dan snorted. "Let's go."

Back at the strong man's trailer, Dan brought a packet of papers from a drawer. Sure enough, it included a letter with the fancy, embossed letterhead of a New York City talent agency. The letter and the envelope's postmark confirmed the time and place of Dan's meeting.

"I didn't tell Mickey Barnes where I was going because I wasn't sure Cliffson was going to hire me," Dan explained. "I was worried that if Barnes knew I was job hunting, he might replace me before I was ready to leave. So I told him I had to visit a sick aunt for a few days. Then yesterday, while you were breaking into my trailer, I was checking my mail."

The strong man withdrew a slip of yellow paper from his robe pocket. "This telegram came. Cliffson's offering me the job starting next month. This is the break I've been waiting for. I've been with this show eight years. Eight years living in this lousy trailer, working six days a week. I'm sick of it. And I'm finished with steroids. They're out of my life. As Cliffson's trainer, I'll steer clear of them. You know how squeaky clean and wholesome his public image is. If he thought I was on steroids, he'd fire me in a New York minute. Believe me, I'm turning over a new leaf. You can even watch me get rid of these. I don't need them anymore."

The Hardys watched Dan dispose of the pills by upending the bottles into the fly-infested garbage bins behind the chow tent. As they walked away, Frank said, "Do you think he'll keep his promise to stay clean?"

"Let's hope so, for his sake," Joe said.

Since show time wasn't for a while, Frank and Joe headed directly for the vet's trailer.

No one answered their knock.

"Probably still out doing his laundry," Joe guessed.

"In that case he could be gone for a while," Frank said. "That gives us plenty of time to look around his trailer."

Joe stepped close to the door and Frank stood lookout. When the lock clicked, Joe grasped the knob.

"Careful," Frank warned. "Remember the birds."

"How could I forget them?" Joe said.

Slipping in through a narrow opening, Frank and Joe closed the door behind them.

The birds seemed calmer than they had the night before. Perched along chair backs, counter tops, and cabinets, they chirped louder as Frank and Joe came in, but settled down again when Frank closed the door.

"What exactly are we looking for?" Joe said.

"Anything suspicious looking or odd," Frank said.

"Odd," Joe repeated. "You mean besides a tiny trailer full of birds perched everywhere in sight. Oops—*eesh!* Watch where you put your hands. These things aren't housebroken."

Frank and Joe searched the trailer, hunting through drawers and cabinets, in the closet, and under the bed.

"Watch it, bird," Joe said at one point, nudging a canary gently aside with his finger.

Ten minutes later Frank stooped in front of the bureau. "Hey . . ." he said slowly.

Tucked in the back of a clothes drawer he had found a small soldering iron, a pair of needle-nose pliers, a fine metal file, and a dozen pea-sized open metal rings.

"What do you think this is for?" Joe asked.

"Beats me," Frank said. "It sure doesn't look like vet stuff. These little rings look almost like earring hoops, but not quite," he added, putting them back.

When Frank had closed the drawer, he turned and surveyed the room. "Well, this was a waste of time. There's not a single thing that tells us anything. Let's get going."

"Wait a sec, Frank. Check this out." Joe stood beside the infrared breeding lamps.

Frank joined his brother.

Beneath the large red bulb one of the tiny eggs

was jiggling slightly. As Frank and Joe watched, a tiny crack appeared.

"Cool," Joe said.

Moments later a pin-size hole appeared and then, a second after that, a tiny beak passed through it. The crack widened, and a piece of shell fell away. Frank and Joe had seen eggs hatch before, but they still found it fascinating.

Soon a small wet chick, its head seeming much too big for its body, lay panting among the pieces of broken eggshell.

"You can actually see his heart beating inside his chest," Joe said. "But look, we'd better get going."

But Frank continued to stare. "Wait, Joe." Frank peered at the hatchling. "Look closely at that bird. There isn't a single other one like it in the whole room."

Chapter
10

"THAT'S WEIRD," Joe said.

"Check out its beak," Frank said. "It's got a hooked beak."

Joe stared down at the fledgling chick. The tiny beak *was* hooked—like a parakeet's. Yet all the other birds fluttering or perched around the room had straight beaks. The canaries' pink ones and the finches' multicolored ones—some white, some shades of purple—all were pointed, cone shaped, and straight.

"You're right," Joe said. "You think their beaks straighten out as they get older?"

"No." Frank shook his head decisively. "Remember that biology report I did last year on birds? I feel as if I know everything there is to know about beaks. Something like that would be impossible."

He peered at the bird more closely. "That chick looks like a tiny parrot. Unless Thurston's figured a way for one breed to lay the eggs of another, something strange is definitely going on here."

"Come to think of it, remember when he knocked over the lamp?" Joe said. "It was exactly when we were looking at these eggs. You think he got scared we might see something we weren't supposed to?"

"Either that or he really wasn't scared at all. With his birds going wild, he'd have the perfect excuse to kick us out."

"But why? What could he be hiding inside an unhatched bird's egg?"

"Illegally trafficking in rare and valuable birds is a federal crime. What if he has a smuggling ring of some kind, and what if Freddie found out?"

"We should definitely talk to him." Joe checked his watch. "Assuming he's in town doing his laundry, he shouldn't be much longer. That bag didn't look that full." But suddenly Joe's brow furrowed. "Wait a minute."

The younger Hardy turned and went into the trailer's tiny bathroom. He returned with a small wicker hamper. Lifting the lid, he showed his brother the contents. "His laundry's still here.

But his toothbrush, razor, and hairbrush are gone—"

"—so maybe he wasn't planning to come back. But would he leave without his trailer?"

"Driving off with it would attract too much attention. He could just hop a local bus into town, then catch a train or bus to any place in the country."

Frank turned toward the door. "He's got a decent head start, but if we get going now, we'd still have a shot at catching up to him."

Frank and Joe rushed out of the trailer, then strode toward the bus stop at the south end of the parade grounds. The posted schedule said the next bus to town wasn't due for forty minutes.

"Too long," Joe said. "It'll give him too big a lead."

Frank turned on his heel. "Come on. I've got an idea."

As Frank and Joe headed toward the show trucks, Frank poked Joe. "There's the one we need."

Seeing the tall, bright red Wheels of Death Stunt Riders tractor-trailer, Joe guessed what his brother had in mind. "If anyone sees us, we'll get fired," Joe said.

Frank climbed into the open rear of the truck. "We're not stealing anything. We're just borrowing a couple of bikes for a little while," he said. "If we head out through the woods in back, no one should see us. This truck doesn't get unloaded until later. I'm sure we'll have the bikes back before anyone even notices they're missing. Now, help me with the ramp."

As Frank and Joe rolled two stunt bikes to the ground, Joe said, "These look awesome. I'll bet they have monster acceleration."

The gleaming twin black-and-silver stunt motorcycles had the knobby tires, suspension, and shock-absorbing seats of dirt bikes but with oversize engines.

"Grab the keys and a pair of helmets off those pegs and let's go," Frank said.

Moments later Frank and Joe were tearing along the fringe of the woods. The bikes *were* fast, but it wasn't until the Hardys reached the blacktop that they saw what the machines really could do. Frank worried that if a police car spotted them wearing their bright red coveralls and silver stunt riders' helmets with orange flames painted on the sides, they would be pulled over for sure. Still, they zipped along at a fast clip, trees skimming past as the bikes ate up the country roads. Soon houses started cropping up, and as Frank and Joe crested a hill, a small town opened up below. The Hardys roared onto the main street until Frank, riding ahead, signaled Joe to pull over.

"Now where to?" Joe asked, once he and Frank had stopped and flipped up their face shields.

"This town looks too small to have a train station. Let's find the bus depot."

Frank asked directions from a passerby, and after revving their engines, Frank and Joe sped off.

Outside a squat, redbrick building with a sign that said Straight Line Transit—The Shortest Distance Between Two Points, Frank and Joe parked, then hurried to the door.

The waiting area was like others in a thousand small towns across the country: orange molded-plastic seats, scenic posters of cities, and a video monitor showing arrival and departure times. Several people looked up as the Hardys came in, but Thurston wasn't among them.

"Excuse me," Frank said to the ticket clerk, a balding, middle-aged man who seemed fascinated by their coveralls and helmets. "Did a man come in in the past half hour or so—short, thin, about forty years old, carrying a white laundry bag?"

"He left on the two o'clock to Houston," the clerk said, trying not to stare. "It just pulled out."

Moments later Frank and Joe were racing out of town toward the interstate. Hunched forward on their souped-up machines, they flew along, Joe now in the lead. There was little traffic as they leaned gently into the curves, then accelerated out of them for extra speed, passing other vehicles.

Soon a silvery glimmer appeared ahead. Joe signaled Frank with two blasts of his horn. Before long, the glimmer became the tall, broad rear of a bus.

The bus was cruising at about sixty miles per hour as Frank and Joe drew up behind it. When he was sure it was safe, Frank flicked on his turn signal and pulled into the other lane. Riding beside the bus, he squinted up at its windows, but he couldn't see anything through them because they were tinted. Frank twisted the throttle, gunned the bike ahead, then pulled smoothly into the bus's lane. Joe joined him. Frank and Joe waved, trying to pull the bus over. Its driver ignored them.

The older Hardy tried a different tactic. He slowed. Joe followed suit. They decelerated to fifty, then forty miles an hour. The bus grew huge in their rearview mirrors. Six feet behind Joe's rear tire, it flashed its high beams and blared its horn, its broad silver grille looking like a stainless-steel wall. But Frank and Joe slowed further—to thirty, then twenty miles per hour.

With no choice but to pull over or run down the two cyclists, the bus driver finally flicked on his right turn signal. Seeing the flashing yellow light and hearing the huge engine shift gears, Joe breathed a sigh of relief.

Once the bus had pulled over, raising a cloud of dust from the dirt shoulder, the Hardys also parked, flicked down their kickstands, whipped off their helmets, and trotted to the bus door, which stood open.

The driver, a large man in a gray uniform shirt, sat looking down at them, his face flushed beneath his black visor.

"What do you think you're doing?" he snapped.

"Sir, we're sorry, but this is an emergency," Frank said, bounding up the steps and feeling the cool air lick his face. "We need to talk with one of your passengers."

"Well, it had *better* be an emergency, for your sake." The driver nodded at his CB radio. "I already called the state police, and they're on their way."

Joe also boarded. The bus wasn't crowded. Only a dozen or so startled passengers stared up at the Hardys.

"Is this a hijacking?" an older woman asked.

"No, ma'am," Joe said. "Please stay calm. We're conducting an investigation." They headed toward the back of the bus and found the circus vet slouched in a seat there.

"Dr. Thurston," Frank said. "Going someplace?"

"I was just taking a short day trip," the vet said.

"So you must have bought a round-trip ticket," Frank said. "Let's see it."

Thurston smiled nervously.

"Listen, mister," the driver said to the vet. "If these guys are bothering you, don't worry. The police'll be here any minute."

"Somehow I think the police are the *last* ones

he wants to see," Joe said. "Step off the bus, Doctor."

On the dirt shoulder, Frank said to Thurston, "Congratulations. You pulled off an ornithological miracle. Getting finches and canaries to lay parrot eggs. Maybe you'd like to tell us how you did it—that is, before you explain it to the U.S. Fish and Wildlife Service. Aren't they in charge of regulating importation of exotic birds?"

"I don't know what you're talking about," the vet said.

"Sure you don't," Frank said. "You just decided to make a run for it out of the blue. What happened? Did Freddie discover your secret? Was he going to turn you in? Is that why you switched the pins on him? If he dies, you know, you'll be facing a murder charge."

"What are you guys, cops?"

"No, but I bet we can have some here in about five minutes if you want to give us a hard time."

"Look, I had nothing to do with Freddie's accident," Thurston said.

"We know somebody tried to kill him and right now it looks as if you've got a pretty good motive," Joe said.

"I swear I didn't do it. You have to believe me. Okay, I admit I've been raising and selling the birds."

"Also known as trafficking in exotic animals," Frank said. "So, tell us about it."

"All right. I-I've been selling birds. The circus

doesn't pay much, and I've been making extra money on the side."

The vet explained that each year when the show traveled through southern Texas, Thurston's accomplices smuggled Mexican parrot eggs across the border inside secret compartments in carefully designed cushioned clothing, baggage, and even inside phony spare car tires, and delivered them to the vet. Thurston hatched the eggs under his heat lamps, then sold the chicks along the circus's travel route.

"So all those birds you keep are just a cover for your business," Joe said. "So you can raise eggs without attracting much attention."

"I'll bet that can be pretty lucrative," Frank said. "How much do parrots sell for on the black market?"

"Military macaws bring a thousand dollars each in the States," Thurston said. "Others—the Mexican parrotlet, the Mexican redheaded Amazon—vary with the bird."

"How about that equipment—the soldering iron, pliers, metal rings, and fine-toothed metal file?" Frank said. "What are you doing, banding the birds with them?"

The vet admitted he was. He explained that all exotic birds imported legally into the country wore small, solid, unremovable metal leg bands that were put on them when they were two to three weeks old. As the birds grew, their feet became too big for the bands to be slipped over, so the bands showed they had been raised disease free and had passed through U.S. Customs quarantine. But Thurston put phony bands onto birds smuggled in illegally, then squeezed the bands closed, soldered the gap, and filed the spot down smooth to make the rings look as if they'd been put on legally.

"Getting back to Freddie," Frank said. "He discovered your little sideline business, didn't he?"

"I was in my trailer dealing with one of my clients along the route one day, and Freddie came barging in. He saw a couple of eggs and a wad of money."

"So you arranged his so-called accident to make sure he didn't tell anyone," Frank said.

"Absolutely not," the vet insisted. "I told you, I had nothing to do with that. Sure, I was worried he might tell somebody. We were pretty good friends, but he avoided me after that. I wasn't sure what he was going to do, but I never would have hurt him. I can't stand violence. I don't know what I'd have done if he tried to turn me in—probably run, just as I did today. But then Freddie had his accident and it looked as if things would work out. I was safe again—that is, until you two came asking questions. Then I panicked and made a run for it."

"Leaving all your little beauties behind," Frank said, "including the parrot eggs. As for your motor home, you just had to sacrifice it.

There was no way for you to drive off without attracting attention."

When a pair of state police cars arrived and the troopers heard the Hardy brothers' story, they drove Thurston away, heading back to his trailer to confiscate the eggs and collect the leg bands, soldering iron, and other tools as evidence. Frank was relieved the police hadn't asked about his and Joe's motorcycles.

"So what do you think, Joe?" Frank asked, as they straddled their bikes. "Did Thurston pull the pin swap?"

"No," Joe said. "I believe him about not being the violent type."

"All right, let's get back and see if we can flush out the real killer," Frank said. When they returned to the circus, they left the stunt bikes parked beside the red truck so it would look as if they'd just been unloaded. Then Frank and Joe spent the rest of the day and evening tending to their duties.

It was eleven-thirty by the time they finished loading the last truck. Most of the other workers were already in the semi as the Hardys climbed aboard, glad for the flickering candle to undress by.

" 'Night, Joe," Frank said, climbing up into his bunk.

"See you in the morning," Joe answered, crouching down to his sleeping space. In the gloom, he slipped his bare feet beneath the scratchy blanket. He was tired and was just drifting off when something moved near his feet. Thinking he must be dreaming, he probed with his toe and felt a strange object with a rough, hard surface. Then it moved. Joe jerked his feet away and flipped the blanket aside.

In the weak yellow light he saw a huge Gila monster, with its telltale orange and black markings. The foot-and-a-half-long lizard stared at Joe with glittering black eyes, its body tense and alert.

Suddenly it ran at Joe, scurrying across the lumpy mattress on its short, squat legs. The poisonous lizard's mouth hung open wide, its pointy white teeth coming straight at Joe's bare toes.

Chapter

11

JOE SPRANG FROM HIS BUNK, snatched up the two mattress corners, and folded the thin straw pad in half, trapping the lizard. With the angry creature hissing inside, he lifted the whole mattress and ran for the sliding door. He kicked it open, leaned out, and shook the lizard out over an open metal trash can. Then Joe jumped down and slammed the lid closed.

"Joe?" Frank called from the semi. Other workers were grumbling, and Joe could hear the Gila monster's claws inside the can. The next moment Frank appeared at the open doorway barefoot, his shirt hanging out of his pants.

"What's going on?" he asked.

Joe beckoned toward the side of the truck. "Come on over here."

107

After Joe had described finding his unwelcome bed partner, Frank shook his head. "And you're sure it was a Gila monster?"

"See for yourself," Joe said. The Hardys had been out west plenty of times and knew a Gila monster when they saw one.

"That's okay, I'll take your word for it," Frank said. He knew that when they bit they didn't let go. The poison-injecting teeth were in back and Gilas held on as long as it took to inject their victim. "Those things are like lizard pit bulls."

"Thanks, I feel lots better," Joe said. "But the question is, how'd it get in there? I mean, for it to have climbed the ladder and gotten into my bunk without anyone seeing it seems incredible."

"Joe, Gila monsters don't even live in this part of the country. They're from the Southwest. Someone had to get it from somewhere nearby to put it in your bunk—maybe to end our investigation? They take you out and bang, the investigation comes to a grinding halt. First the tiger, and now this.

"All right, let's think about where someone could get a Gila monster and who the person is who's most used to handling all kinds of animals."

"I guess that'd be Willie Thurston, the vet."

"Uh-huh. Except Thurston would have had to put the lizard there before leaving for town. Meaning he had to count on it staying in your bunk all day. Not a very dependable plan. And anyway, why put it there *and* leave? He'd try either to get us off the investigation *or* make a run for it, not both." Frank shook his head as he looked at his brother. "Who else can you think of who's used to handling poisonous reptiles?"

"Sinjay Darbar. Maybe we should find out if he has any pet Gila monsters and whether any are missing." Joe glanced at his watch. "I'd be surprised if he wasn't in his trailer asleep at this hour."

But as Frank and Joe made their way through the dark field, they saw that most of the performers' trailers were already gone. Only a few equipment trucks remained, idling with rumbling engines, their headlights shining on the trees. At the spot where Darbar's trailer had been, Frank and Joe found only tire ruts.

"We'll have to save this for tomorrow," Frank said. He checked his watch. "Come on. It's past midnight. Let's get back to the semi before someone closes the door and they leave without us."

The next morning, though the Hardys would have liked to speak with Sinjay Darbar first thing, they had their chores to tend to. At yet another anonymous public fairgrounds outside another nameless town, they helped unload heavy wooden ring curbs, the trapeze artists' net, and Marlin Randolf's disappearing box, from which his magic act assistant would appear to vanish, thanks to a series of tunnels beneath the platform. There were also the huge hoops, balls, and pedestals that were part of the cat act and the cushioned catapults and floor pads of the acrobats' routine.

Just as the Hardys were about to begin the last chore before their afternoon break, a pulley snapped, delaying things as all the workers had to wait until it was fixed before they could finish their work. It wasn't until early afternoon, just before the first show, that Frank and Joe got a chance to visit the snake charmer.

"You again?" Darbar said.

"We want to know about Gila monsters," Frank said.

"What about them?" Darbar asked.

"Do you have any and where are they?" Frank asked.

"Yes," Darbar said. "I have Gila monsters, but this is none of your business. First you break into my home, and now you start questioning me about my animals."

Joe said, "Somebody put a Gila monster in my bunk, and it almost bit me. How many do you have and where are they?"

"I have three, but there's one missing," Darbar said. "Sometimes the towners steal them for pets, until they get a finger bitten off. I thought maybe that's what happened. Now I think maybe one of your fellow workers did it as a sick prank. Why don't you ask them and leave me alone? Can't you see I'm preparing for a show?"

"Where were you yesterday from, say, three in the afternoon until eleven last night?" Joe asked.

"When I wasn't performing I was cooking. Mondays I prepare big pots of chicken biryani and mulligatawny soup for the coming week. Shahela helps me. She was there, too. But enough questions. You're accusing me, aren't you? You have some nerve coming around again. Now, get out of here at once before I call Mr. Barnes."

Joe said, "Fine, but until you can prove otherwise, I'm figuring you put that Gila in my bunk and I'm waiting for an answer why."

Frank and Joe walked away.

"Ladies and gentlemen," boomed the ringmaster's amplified voice from beneath the big top.

"Come on, Joe," Frank said. "Let's get back. The show's starting."

Frank and Joe walked at a quick pace across the fairgrounds, which were practically deserted now that the show had begun. The sound of calliope music escorted them to the big tent.

"Well, his alibi is Shahela—not exactly a disinterested party," Frank said.

"True, but somehow I don't think he'd put her in the position of having to lie for him," Joe said. "I bet they *were* preparing that food."

"If that's true, and what he said about the Gila monster disappearing is, too, then anyone could have planted it in your bunk."

Entering the tent, Frank and Joe found the

stands packed and the show under way. In the introductory procession, all the clowns marched to center ring, faced the crowd on all sides, and sang the national anthem. As Frank and Joe stood at attention, their eyes played over the performers. When the music and singing ended, Frank said, "Joe, I don't see Bobo Rosyberk, do you?"

Joe scanned the crowd. "Nope. I wonder where he is?"

The show opener began, and the acrobats bounded in from the wings. The crowd cheered, and Frank and Joe grabbed their performing props, including the acrobats' cushioned seesaws, from which they would catapult to stand on each other's shoulders. During the act Frank and Joe returned to the side to watch. The clowns stood nearby.

"Where's Bobo?" Tiny Winston said to another clown. "We're on soon. Shouldn't he be here by now?"

"Should be," another clown said. "He's probably just running late again. Sometimes he just dozes off."

"You think I should go get him?" Winston asked.

"Only if you want your head bit off. That ornery old coot's no one to mess with. You're better off getting Mickey Barnes. He'll take care of Bobo better than you could."

For the next ten minutes Frank and Joe carried

sections of the cat cage into ring number two. Each of the eighty interlocking pieces of vertical steel bars, over which a net would be stretched when they were in place, stood eight feet tall and three feet wide and weighed seventy pounds. By the time they were all unloaded from the truck and carried into the tent, the workers were all sweating heavily.

When Frank and Joe had finished, they moved again to where the clowns were preparing in the wings.

"Still no Bobo," Tiny Winston was saying. "I'll go find Barnes."

Frank turned to Joe. "Let's go check Bobo's trailer."

Frank and Joe made their way across the grounds.

"There," Joe said, spotting the huge trailer parked off to the side.

The Hardys went over to it and listened at the door a moment. They heard the sound of someone moving around inside as if in a hurry. There were rushed footsteps and drawers opening and closing in rapid succession.

"Probably just woke up and saw how late he's running," Joe whispered.

Frank knocked. Abruptly the movement in the trailer stopped. There was complete silence. Frank and Joe looked at each other.

"Try again," Joe said.

Frank knocked again.

"Hello?" he called. "Bobo?"

Still no answer. Frank reached out and gripped the knob. He looked at Joe, mouthed one, two, three, and yanked the door open. Joe bounded in, Frank a half step behind him.

They burst into the room—and stopped short. There stood Bobo Rosyberk, not in his clown costume, but wearing jeans, a short-sleeved shirt, and sneakers. In his left hand he held a worn leather suitcase stuffed to capacity. In his right hand he held a revolver.

"Out of my way," Bobo ordered. "I'll shoot you if I have to." And with that he raised the gun.

"Hey, Bobo. We've already caught this act, remember?" Joe said. He started toward the clown.

"Hold it, Joe," Frank said.

Joe turned and followed Frank's gaze. On the dressing table among the colored wigs, jars of makeup, and false noses, lay Bobo's prop gun, its red Bang! You're Dead! flag sticking out its muzzle.

The big clown thumbed back the hammer on his shiny silver revolver. "Move it," he said in a deep voice as he pointed the gun directly at Joe's chest.

Chapter

12

"NOW, JUST TAKE IT EASY," Joe said, raising his hands slowly and distracting Rosyberk enough for Frank to launch a karate kick that smashed Rosyberk's knuckles and deflected the gun.

Joe sprang forward and grabbed Rosyberk's wrist. Keeping the revolver pointed at the floor, Joe pivoted, wrenching the clown's gun arm sideways. Rosyberk's hand sprang open, and the gun flew from his grasp, clattering across the floor and sliding under the bed.

"Okay, Bobo," Frank said as Joe released the clown's arm and Frank shoved the packed suitcase aside. "Let's talk about the pin swap and Freddie's so-called accident."

Rosyberk stood rubbing his elbow and grimacing. "No. You've got it all wrong. I didn't do a thing to Freddie."

"Of course not," Joe said, eyeing the bulging suitcase. "You just decided to take a little day trip all of a sudden. It's amazing how popular they are lately."

"This has nothing to do with Freddie," Rosyberk said.

"So what *is* your excuse?" Frank said. "And it better be good."

"How about to save my life?" the clown said.

"What are you talking about?" Frank said.

"I got to thinking," the clown continued. "No one could have known ahead of time I'd sprain my ankle and ask Freddie to stand in. That happened at the very last minute, which means whoever swapped those pins wasn't after Freddie. The person was after me."

"You?" Joe said.

"Me. I was the target," the clown said. "It was never Freddie at all. I just happened to get lucky. He subbed so he got hit. But he's a young guy, in good shape. He'll probably be okay. If I'd fallen off that wire, I would've broken my neck. That's why I'm getting out of here now. I'm not waiting around for whoever it was to try again."

The Hardys looked at each other. Much as they hated to admit it, Bobo had a point. They'd been so caught up in trying to prove that Freddie wasn't the victim of an accident, it hadn't occurred to them that he might have been an accidental victim.

"So you pulled a gun on us because you thought we were out to finish the job?" Frank said.

"I was scared," Rosyberk said. "Wouldn't you be? Someone's out to kill you, you're packing your things to get out, and they come busting in the door."

"Where were you headed?" Joe asked.

"Anywhere. I hadn't decided. Just as far from here as I can get."

"But what about your wife—and the trailer?" Joe asked.

"I'd have sent for her later." The clown shrugged. "Or maybe not. Just leave her the trailer and go. Married life hasn't turned out the way I thought it would."

"So who are your enemies?" Joe said. "Who would want to kill you?"

At that moment there was a loud knock at the door. Frank and Joe exchanged a look, and Rosyberk's eyes grew wide. He glanced toward the bed. The gun was still under there. Frank nodded toward the door. "Answer it," he whispered.

Rosyberk hesitated.

"Go ahead," Joe said. "We're here. We've got you covered. Maybe we can finally get to the bottom of this."

The clown cleared his throat, then said in a loud voice, "Who's there?"

After a brief pause the door flew open.

"So you *are* here," a familiar voice shouted. Mickey Barnes stormed in. "You're supposed to be on in five minutes. Why aren't you ringside? I pay you to put on a show, in case you forgot." Seeing the Hardys, Barnes demanded, "And what're you two doing here? Doesn't anybody at this show work?"

"Look, Barnes," Bobo said, reaching for his suitcase. "You're gonna have to get somebody new. I quit."

"What?" Barnes shouted. "What are you talking about? I've got a show to put on. *You've* got a show to put on. You can't just leave."

"Oh, no? You watch me," Bobo said. "Find somebody who doesn't mind people trying to kill him. I'm outta here."

"Are you crazy? I don't know what you're talking about, Bobo, but you can't just walk out, not without giving proper notice. I need time to hire a replacement."

Bobo lifted the suitcase, leaning to one side from its weight. "I'm outta here and that's final."

"Bobo, be reasonable. Just give us one more show," Barnes continued. "I can get someone here to replace you tomorrow."

"Sorry," the clown said, moving toward the door.

"Bobo, I'm warning you," Barnes said. "Walk out on me like this and I'll tell every circus owner and carny boss in North America you let me down. Your name will be mud. No one will ever hire you again.''

The clown paused, one hand on the doorknob.

"Come on," Barnes pleaded. "Just finish up your professional obligation. Tonight's show. That's all. Then you can go wherever you want. Go to the moon for all I care.''

Bobo hesitated. "All right, but this is it—the last show.''

Barnes rushed forward and clapped the clown's back. "That's much better. Now hurry up and get into your costume. You're on in a few minutes.''

As Rosyberk set down his bag, Barnes moved toward the door. "I'll tell Sasha to stretch out her act," he said, "but you get out there as quick as you can.'' He turned to the Hardys. "And you get out there, too. I don't pay people to just stand around, no matter what you may think. I've had complaints about you two already. The next time I have to talk to you, you're both history, understand?'' With that the show boss stormed out the door.

Bobo had pulled off his shirt, revealing another, a striped performance shirt. Taking the curly green wig from its peg and pulling it onto his head, he turned one way, then the other, adjusting it. "I don't know why I agreed to that. Seems like Barnes has always had me over a barrel.'' He grabbed a bag of potato chips from the counter, tore it open, and grabbed a handful.

"Easy, Bobo," Joe said.

"Happens every time I get worked up," the clown said. "I gotta eat." He piled a handful in his mouth.

"We'll look out for you," Frank said.

Bobo opened a jar of whiteface makeup, jabbed two fingers in, then smeared a huge bright gob across his forehead.

"Great. A couple of kids are gonna look out for me. Just what I need— *Yecch!*" Frank and Joe stared as the clown turned and spat the chips onto the floor. "Garlic," he said. "Who bought garlic chips? I hate garlic chips." With that he flung the bag across the room, a comet's tail of chips trailing to the floor.

The clown spun around.

"And don't you two have anything better to do than sit gawking? I've got work to do, and you're ruining my concentration," he snapped.

"You never told us who might be out to get you, Bobo," Joe said. "If we had any clues, we might be able to help you out of this jam."

"Who are you, Dick Tracy?" Rosyberk said. "I thought I told you to get out of here. If you've got something to say, say it after the show. I'll have plenty of time then."

"Come on, Joe," Frank said. "Let's get back to work. If he doesn't want our help, we can't force him."

As Frank and Joe headed back to the big top, Joe said, "Looks like we're back at square one."

"The more I see of him, the more I understand why someone would want to get rid of Bobo the clown," Frank said.

"Maybe it was clown rivalry after all," Joe said.

"At least we know it wasn't Freddie," Frank said. "But it could have been any of the other clowns."

As Frank and Joe entered the tent, Mickey Barnes, standing in the wings near the flap, rushed up to them. "One of you grab a broom and get ready to help sweep up Sasha's snowstorm."

"I'll do it," Frank said to his brother. "You keep an eye on Bobo's trailer door. Make sure he doesn't try to make a last-minute run for it."

"And also that no one pays him a surprise visit," Joe said.

The Hardys took turns watching Bobo's trailer throughout Sasha's show.

"She's really stretching out her act," Joe finally said.

It was true. The horsewoman wasn't smiling as she had at the beginning of her act ten minutes before. Now she was grimacing as she stood on her white horse while it circled the ring. The clowns in the wings shifted their feet impatiently. Mickey Barnes anxiously lit a cigar and puffed thick clouds of blue smoke, checking his watch every thirty seconds, his brow furrowed.

As Sasha made yet another pass, Frank and Joe saw her shoot Barnes an exasperated look. The scowling show boss turned toward his clowns.

"Give him one more minute," Barnes said. "If he's not here by then, go in without him and cut the football sketch." The show boss glared back toward Bobo's trailer. "I said I'd blackball him if he did this, and so help me, I will."

"Frank," Joe said, his voice low, "I haven't seen Bobo leave, and I haven't seen anyone go into his trailer. There's no way it could be taking him this long. Let's go see what's keeping him."

As soon as Mickey Barnes turned his back, Frank and Joe slipped out of the tent. They rushed across the field to Bobo's trailer, and Frank knocked.

There was no answer.

"Not again," Joe muttered. "I'm not up for an instant replay."

"You think he sneaked out the back while we weren't looking?"

"No way. We had the door covered and there's no way he could squeeze through one of those tiny windows."

"Careful," Joe said. "He's still got that gun."

Frank eased the door open. "Bobo?"

Frank and Joe stepped in and stopped short, staring.

Rosyberk was leaning forward in his chair, sprawled on his dressing table in full costume.

The big clown's green wig sat askew on his head. Where the left side of his face lay pressed on the table, his whiteface had smeared the surface. His eyes were wide open and glassy, and he looked like an enormous, lifeless doll.

Chapter

13

FRANK RUSHED OVER and grasped the clown's wrist. "No pulse, Joe," he said. "Let's get him to the floor." Frank and Joe eased the big man off the chair and laid him down. Frank pressed two fingers to Rosyberk's neck while placing his ear to the huge chest. "Nothing," Frank said.

"I'll get the doctor," Joe said, and raced out the door.

Left alone, Frank studied the stricken man. Though the left side of his face was covered with the white pancake makeup he had been applying, the other side, still bare, was a pale, waxy yellow. Frank held his hand over the man's eyes, then took his hand away. The pupils remained fixed and didn't change with the light at all. A bad sign, Frank thought grimly.

Running feet could be heard outside.

"Right in here," Joe called, flinging open the door. Dr. Greene, a short woman with dark hair and wearing a white jacket, rushed in behind him, stethoscope in hand.

"There's no pulse," Frank said. "He's not breathing, and his pupils are fixed."

The doctor checked the vital signs for herself. She moved quickly and surely. But after some moments, she grimly, gently, lowered Bobo's arm to his side.

"I'm afraid he's gone," the doctor said somberly. "Poor Bobo. I've known him since I joined the show. Were you with him when he collapsed?"

"I'd say ten to fifteen minutes before," Frank said.

"Well, I don't see any signs of external injury—no blood from a knife or bullet wound, no obvious trauma from a blow to the head."

"Actually, we were watching his trailer the whole time, and no one even came to the door," Joe said.

"Hmm," the doctor replied. "Tell me, when you were with him did he complain of chest pains or shortness of breath? Did he seem dizzy or disoriented? Did spittle form at his mouth?"

"Not at all," Frank said.

"Well, it could have hit him suddenly. A massive heart attack can kill almost instantly. I just hope he didn't suffer much."

"You think it was a heart attack?" Joe asked.

"I've been warning Bobo for years to lose some weight, cut back on his alcohol, and ditch those cigars. At his age, with his high blood pressure and his short temper, he's been a prime candidate for as long as I've known him. It looks as if it finally caught up with him."

"You should know that just a few minutes ago he told us he thought someone was trying to kill him," Frank said. "And now he's dead."

"Well," the doctor said, "with no signs of trauma and knowing his medical history as I do, I'd say everything points to a heart attack."

"Given the circumstances, I'd recommend an autopsy," Frank said.

"You would, hmm?" The doctor raised her eyebrows. "You're making recommendations to me about medical matters? Don't you think you're overstepping your boundaries?"

"We may work as laborers," Frank said, "but we've also been involved in dozens of criminal investigations."

After Frank explained their real purpose in joining the show, the doctor slowly nodded.

"So, you don't think Freddie Felix's fall was an accident and you suspect Bobo's death may be related?" the doctor asked.

"Absolutely," Frank said.

"Which is why an autopsy would probably be a good idea," Joe added.

The doctor pursed her lips, deliberating. "I really don't think it's necessary. Tell it to the police if you're so convinced there's foul play. For now I'm ruling it a heart attack."

"We'd still like to look around a little," Joe said.

"Fellas, do you see marks on the body? Signs of violence or a struggle? I know this place is a mess, but it doesn't look as if there was a fight or a burglar ransacked it for valuables. Anyway, you said yourself you didn't see anyone near the trailer."

Frank and Joe frowned.

"Now, I'm sorry about Bobo, I truly am," the doctor said. "He wasn't the most pleasant person in the world, but it's still a shame. But as for an autopsy—I have other things to attend to, and I seriously doubt the local authorities in a place like this are going to run a postmortem on a stranger who happened to die while passing through." The doctor moved to Bobo's bed and pulled off a sheet that was hanging half on the floor. She spread it over Bobo's body.

"I wouldn't want anyone to wander in and see him like this, especially Celina. Now I'm going to call the police and the coroner's office, so if you'll excuse me . . ."

"Come on, Joe," Frank said.

The Hardys left the clown's trailer and headed back for the big top.

"So what are the chances that was a massive heart attack?" Joe asked, looking at his brother.

Frank shook his head. "All the stress of packing up, dealing with us, then trying to get ready for the show while thinking someone was out to kill him could have brought it on."

"It could have," Joe said, "but my hunch is there's more to it."

"Mine, too."

"So, now what?" Joe said.

The sound of applause drifted to them from the big top. "Now we get back to work," Frank said. "But the first chance we get, let's hit Bobo's trailer to hunt for clues."

Returning to the tent, Frank and Joe tended to their chores. But Joe's mind was a million miles away as he mulled over the latest lethal development.

The clown act had begun, minus one clown, and before long its abbreviated version ended. Frank, Joe, and the other workers rushed in, collected the props lying around the ring, and rushed out. Next came the cat act. As the band struck up "Hold That Tiger," Gus drove out in a little locomotive pulling six cages on wheels. The mini-train weaved back and forth like a giant snake, to the audience's delight. But Joe hardly noticed, he was so wrapped up in his thoughts.

The tigers leaped through rings of fire, balanced on balls, and lined up in order of size. Toward the end of the act one stubborn young male that had had to be threatened with the whip to obey Buck's commands suddenly whirled and charged its trainer with a show of fangs, batting the chair from Buck's hand clear across the cage. The audience gasped, but Buck whipped out his revolver and fired several deafening shots above his head, bringing the tiger back to submission as he did during every performance. That particular tiger was the best trained of all, Buck's personal favorite, able to make its attack look truly deadly.

The crowd cheered.

The shots had jarred Joe back to his surroundings, and for a moment he thought about the genuine tiger attack on Frank. If Frank hadn't snatched the tranquilizer gun and shot the tiger as it charged, and if he hadn't 'aimed accurately, and for that matter, if the tranquilizer hadn't kicked in immediately . . .

Suddenly Joe blinked. The tranquilizer gun. Joe looked over at it. When the heavy dose of tranquilizer had kicked in, the tiger had staggered as if dizzy and had seemed disoriented. Its breathing grew labored, and just before it collapsed, spittle had formed at its mouth. Those were the exact symptoms Dr. Greene had asked if Bobo had shown.

Was there any connection?

Joe edged to where Frank stood and told him his thoughts.

"I want to take another look in Bobo's trailer," Joe added. "We've got a few minutes until the magic act. We can be back in time if we hurry."

Slipping out the big top's side flap, the Hardys hurried back to the dilapidated trailer. As they approached, a white coroner's van was just leaving. They waited for it to drive off, and then for a tired-looking policeman to climb into his cruiser and follow. Then they went up to the trailer door and found it unlocked.

"Frank," Joe said when they were inside, "what if someone shot him with a tranquilizer dart with a heavy enough dose not just to knock him out but to kill him? There wouldn't be a bullet wound or the noise of a gunshot. In fact, if Bobo managed to call out, his symptoms might even be like those of a heart attack. They could have shot him through the window, say. If they were standing in the woods—"

"Except the window's closed," Frank interrupted, "and locked from the inside." The Hardys double-checked to be sure there were no holes through the glass.

"Anyway," Frank said, "there were no darts on the body, and I don't see any on the floor that might have come loose."

"Mmm," Joe said. "Well, another dead end, I guess." He turned toward the door. Something crunched underfoot. A potato chip from the bag Bobo had flung to the floor. Joe picked the bag up. "He really was hot tempered, wasn't he?"

"You can say that again," Frank replied.

Joe took the half-full bag toward an overflowing wastebasket. "It's a shame to waste these, but I'm not a big garlic fan either." He glanced idly at the label. "That's funny. I thought he said these were garlic chips. 'Potatoes, corn oil, cottonseed oil, salt . . .'" Joe looked up from the ingredients list. "This doesn't mention garlic or garlic flavoring at all."

But Frank was listening to music filtering in through the open door. "Hear that? It's our cue for the magic act. We'd better get back." He moved toward the door. But seeing his brother still standing deep in thought, Frank asked, "You coming?"

"Just a second," Joe said.

"Well, don't be long," Frank warned. And with that he hurried out.

Joe stood holding the bag. He raised it to his nose and sniffed. No garlic smell as far as he could tell. He took a chip out, eyed it closely. Should he taste it? He decided not to and set the bag aside.

Joe turned toward the table, thinking about how he and Frank had found Bobo: pitched forward across the makeup table, preparing for his act. The clown's costume had been half on, and his makeup had been half applied. The green wig had sat askew on his head. Joe saw the wig now on the floor, where it had slipped off when Frank and he had lowered Bobo from his chair. Joe reached down to pick it up. The strands didn't feel like real hair but like plastic. He dropped it onto the table. He looked at the other things on the table. Nothing he hadn't seen before. He picked up the jar of whiteface and began to turn it in his hands. Then a noise sounded from behind him, in the direction of the door.

Joe started to turn and glimpsed something coming fast toward his head. He raised his arm, but too late. He felt a sharp blow to his temple, and then everything went black.

Chapter

14

"JOE! JOE! Can you hear me?"

Joe opened his eyes and Frank's face gradually came into focus. Joe realized he was lying on his back.

"Are you okay?" Frank asked.

"I—I think so— *Ouch!*" Joe raised his hand and felt a lump on the side of his head. It was tender to the touch.

"What happened?" Frank asked.

"Someone whacked me," Joe said. "How long have I been out?"

"Just a few minutes. When you didn't come to the big top, I came right back. Did you see who it was?"

Joe shook his head. "Did you see anyone when you came in?"

"Negative," Frank said. "What were you doing, anyway?" Frank helped his brother to his feet.

"Just poking around some more," Joe said, steadying himself. He noticed the wigs were on the floor and a small makeup bottle lay on its side, no doubt knocked over when he hit the table.

"If you're okay, we'd better get back before Mickey Barnes notices we're AWOL again," Frank said.

Joe nodded. "Wait a second. I had a jar of whiteface in my hand when I got hit. Now I don't see it." Joe scanned the floor, peering under the makeup table and even the bed. "It's gone. Frank, whoever hit me took it."

"Why would anyone steal a jar of whiteface?" Frank asked.

"I don't know, but I'd been holding it, thinking of Bobo tasting garlic in chips that didn't have any, and, hey, it just occurred to me. What if someone laced the chips with something that tasted like garlic but was really poison?"

"Poison that tastes like garlic?" Frank asked doubtfully.

"Why not? Cyanide tastes like bitter almonds. There might be some poisonous chemical that tastes like garlic."

"Well, I guess it's possible."

"Look, there's one way to tell for sure. Let's check with Dr. Greene."

*   *   *

Dr. Greene opened the door of her RV camper. Seeing her visitors, she said, "Any closer to solving the mystery of who killed our heart-attack victim?"

"We may be," Joe said. "And you may be able to help us. Do you know of any poisons that taste like garlic?"

"Let's see . . . garlic." After a moment the doctor shook her head. "I can't think of any. Cyanide tastes like bitter almonds, of course, but as for garlic"—she shrugged—"nothing specific comes to mind."

"You're sure?" Joe asked.

"Sorry."

Frank turned to his brother. "Who knows, Joe, maybe Bobo burped some up from lunch." Frank paused. "Come to think of it, I remember him tearing open a brand-new sealed package. The chips couldn't have been poisoned. Whatever tasted like garlic must have come from somewhere else."

"Wait a second," Dr. Greene said.

The Hardys turned.

"You know, there is one chemical that comes to mind when you mention garlic. DMSO."

"The stuff that athletes sometimes use?" Joe asked.

"Correct. Dimethyl sulfoxide. DMSO for short," the doctor said. She reached for a reference book and quickly consulted it. "Yes, here it is. DMSO's unique side effect is that when applied topically to the epidermis, it makes one imagine the taste of garlic in one's mouth."

"When applied topically to the epidermis," Frank repeated. "You mean when you rub it on your skin?"

"That's right," the doctor said. "DMSO is absorbed through the skin instantly."

"I know athletes sometimes massage it into their muscles after a workout. It increases blood circulation," Frank said.

"Well, that's what some people think, but it's really not true," Dr. Greene said. "All it does is cause a tingling sensation because it's absorbed so fast. But some people find that refreshing." The doctor closed her book. "I don't know whether or not that helps you, but you're going to have to excuse me now. I have some paperwork to take care of for the police and coroner."

"Come on, Joe," Frank said, pulling on his brother's arm. "Let's get back to the tent."

Striding briskly back to the big top, Joe said, "You know, I think all the pieces we need are here. We just have to fit them together."

Entering the tent, Frank and Joe saw that the magic act had already begun.

Suddenly Mickey Barnes came barreling up to them, tapping his wristwatch with his finger.

"Where have you been?" he demanded. "Don't you have a job to do? Doc Greene just told me Bobo had a heart attack. He's *dead*. Now, don't you think I have enough to worry about without constantly looking after you two? I want to see both of you in my trailer right after the show."

When the show boss had stalked off, Frank said to his brother, "Somehow, I don't think he's going to offer us a raise."

As the magician performed his act, Joe's thoughts raced. He was still trying to piece together the details of Bobo's death.

The clown had died at his dressing table, having just complained of tasting garlic in potato chips that had no garlic in them. But DMSO caused the sensation of a garlic taste. If Bobo had applied DMSO to his skin, he would have *thought* the chips were garlic flavored, Joe reasoned. But what if Bobo didn't know he was rubbing on DMSO, because someone had mixed it into his whiteface? But would that be enough to kill him? Of course not. Unless something else was mixed in too—some poison. Or a deadly dose of the cat tranquilizer, which was handy enough.

Of course. The pieces fit. Someone had murdered Bobo by mixing DMSO with a lethal dose of the big cat tranquilizer, then adding the deadly mixture to Bobo's whiteface. When Bobo applied the makeup, his skin absorbed the DMSO-tranquilizer mixture instantly, delivering a lethal dose to his system. The theory also explained why the killer returned to steal the jar and why, seeing

Joe holding it, the murderer knocked Joe out to recover the incriminating evidence.

Unfortunately, Joe still didn't know why the killer had struck, or who the killer was. Whoever it was might still be prowling around or might have gotten far enough away to never be caught.

A loud drum roll pulled Joe from his thoughts.

Marlin Randolf was about to do his colored-water trick. Standing in his tuxedo, a glossy black cape over his shoulders and his wand in his hand, the magician faced the table with the three crystal pitchers of clear liquid.

As the crowd watched, Randolf raised the wand and tapped the edge of each pitcher twice—sharply enough for the piercing ring of crystal to carry to the farthest seats. Joe, standing close, saw that with each tap a tiny pellet dropped from the specially rigged wand to fall into the liquid. The tablets were too small for the crowd to see. Formulated to be time-released, the pills had no effect right away.

But as Randolf stepped back and suddenly leveled the wand sharply at the middle pitcher, the contents of all three turned color in sequence—the first red, the second white, and the third, not emerald green but blue, making for a patriotic tribute.

As the crowd oohed and aahed, then applauded, Joe had to admit the illusion was effective. Randolf had obviously adjusted the mix so the green was now blue. Just then Joe had a thought. If

Randolf knew enough to mix his own chemicals for illusions, would he know how to use DMSO to deliver poison? And if he did, could he be connected to Bobo Rosyberk's heart attack?

Joe stared as the magician took his bows. There was only one way to find out, Joe thought. Run a little test. As the band struck up "That Old Black Magic," the cue for Randolf's grand finale, the disappearing-woman trick, Joe quickly made his way to his brother.

"Frank, I think Randolf might be connected to Rosyberk's death. He's the only one we know around here who can mix chemicals, right?" Joe said.

"Except Dr. Greene," Frank answered.

"Right. So he could have used the DMSO to deliver a fatal dose of tranquilizer," Joe said. "If I can get close to him for a second, I think I can run a test."

"How close do you need to be?" Frank asked.

"Close enough to touch him," Joe said.

"Leave it to me," Frank said. "His final prop's the disappearing box. Help me carry it in."

"Sounds good. I just need to do one more thing first. I'll meet you."

As Joe hurried off, Frank wasted no time moving to the tall, coffin-shaped silver box.

The crowd was still applauding as several workers carried away the colored pitchers.

"Hey," Frank said to two workers who were

about to lift the box. "Take five, you guys. Joe and I will get this."

"Fine with me," said the first worker, stepping aside. But the second hesitated.

"I always take her out," he said.

Frank held up his hand. "We'll handle it this time. Trust us." He stepped in front of the man and bent to grab one end of the box.

"What's going on here?" sounded a familiar voice.

Frank looked up to see Mickey Barnes.

Joe, meanwhile, had crossed to the other side of the ring, where the clowns stood.

"Hey, Tiny," Joe said, stepping in close to the clown. "I'm sorry about this, but it's an emergency." And before Tiny could react, Joe reached up and wiped his index finger across the startled clown's forehead.

"What—" Tiny blurted, his eyes wide with surprise. But Joe was already turning and striding back toward Frank.

Joe held his index finger, bright with shiny white greasepaint, low at his side.

"I don't know what's got into you," Mickey Barnes was saying to Frank as Joe came up, "but you're fired." The show boss turned and saw Joe. "Both of you—I want you both out of here."

"No problem," Joe said. "Just give us a few minutes first. Ready, Frank?"

Before the incredulous show boss could object,

Frank and Joe lifted the long, cumbersome box and started toward center ring.

Randolf was still taking bows as Frank and Joe came up behind him. Joe came first, walking backward, the box at his stomach. He kept his pancaked finger apart from the rest. Joe stepped backward onto the brightly painted ring curb, then stepped down. But as Frank reached it, he kicked the wooden curb loudly and pretended to trip. Stumbling forward, he shoved the box hard. It jammed Joe in the stomach, and he grunted and fell backward, dropping his end and bumping into the magician so they both went down. The crowd burst into laughter. Joe reached out and helped Randolf to his feet. The magician flashed Joe a furious scowl but didn't notice as Joe's pancaked finger left a bright smear of whiteface on his wrist.

"You idiot," Randolf said below his breath. "What's the matter with you?"

"Sorry," Joe whispered. Quickly he and Frank righted the box, standing it on its end. Then Frank and Joe hurried out of the ring to the sidelines on the side opposite from where Mickey Barnes stood glaring at them.

Joe folded his arms to watch the rest of the act. And to watch especially for the moment when Marlin would notice the smear of pancake.

Out came Randolf's assistant, a smiling young woman in a red sequined dress and high heels. The crowd applauded. Randolf, also smiling, opened one of the box's sides as if it were a door, and began to usher her inside.

As Randolf raised his wand, his smile suddenly froze. A look of pure terror crossed his face and he gasped. Joe was watching closely. Randolf whipped out a colorful silk kerchief and brushed frantically at the white smudge on his skin. He seemed as panicked as if his life were at stake. He didn't seem to notice or care that thousands of people were staring. When finally he seemed satisfied, he looked up and his eyes met Joe's, staring straight at him. Joe knew exactly why Randolf was in a panic.

Randolf looked quickly left, then right, like a cornered animal. Whipping his hand from beneath his cape, the magician raised his fist overhead and hurled a handful of pellets to the ground.

As they struck, each flashed and popped like a firecracker, emitting thick green smoke. Within seconds a blinding, choking, pale green cloud billowed across the ring, and the magician disappeared.

Chapter

15

JOE GOT A LUNGFUL of the acrid smoke and felt as if a clamp were gripping his chest. His legs buckled, and he sank to his knees. He tried to stand, but it was all he could do just to keep breathing. Frank, standing at the edge of the ring, saw the noxious smoke wasn't only choking Joe and providing a cover for Randolf to escape, it was also upsetting the animals. The elephants' trainers were struggling to control the huge beasts as they nervously stamped their feet and, looking wild-eyed, started lumbering away from the ring toward the crowd.

The big cats were also upset, loping briskly around their cage and growling nervously as Jim Buck, who must also have gotten a choking dose of the smoke, staggered along, coughing, his head bent to his arm, feeling for the cage door but having trouble finding it.

Frank drew a deep breath, held it, and raced toward the elephants. The smoke stung his eyes and, as they closed to slits, he grimaced. Choosing the nearest elephant, he ran at it full speed, then leaped, snatching at the fringed edge of the heavy red velvet cape across its back. He missed and hit the side of the elephant hard. He jumped again. This time his fingers closed on the thick material. He yanked hard with all his weight, and the cape came down off the animal's wrinkled gray hide. Frank raced to the smoking pellets and flung the big cape across them. Then he darted to Queen Sasha's huge fans.

Snatching up the heavy electrical cables and the long, industrial-grade extension cords, Frank plugged them in. The big-bladed fans came to life and started to disperse the suffocating cloud.

Frank saw Randolf climbing into the disappearing box, no doubt planning to escape through the tunnel beneath the platform. Frank grabbed the magician and dragged him out of the box. They both went down hard, Frank eating dirt.

Randolf kicked Frank in the shoulder and scrambled to his feet. But Frank was only a step behind and, tackling Randolf again, brought them both down once more. As they grappled, something tumbled from beneath the magician's cape—a jar of clown's whiteface, which rolled across the dirt.

"Help," Randolf called. "Celina."

Randolf's cry surprised Frank. Why would the magician expect help from Bobo Rosyberk's wife? Then a hiss sounded near Frank's ear, followed by a loud *thock* inches from his face. Something tugged hard at his shirtsleeve, near the shoulder. Twisting, Frank saw a long, silver-bladed throwing knife whose tip had pierced his coveralls and embedded itself deeply into the wooden disappearing box.

As Randolf scurried away and scrambled to his feet, Frank saw, through the dissipating smoke, Celina Stiletto standing just twenty feet away. In her left hand she held two more knives and in her right, a third, which she held by its tip, raised and poised to throw. Then her hand whipped down just as a blur passed Frank.

Joe scooped up a wooden ring curb and shouted, "Freeze, Frank." He blocked Celina's throw, and a second knife struck the wood with another solid *thwack* and stayed there quivering. Joe kept moving, rushing at Celina with the ring curb as a shield. She raised another deadly blade but moved backward, tripped on one of the curbs behind her, and fell. Two powerful women acrobats rushed forward and seized her arms.

Frank yanked hard on his uniform sleeve and tore it free of the knife. He lunged at Randolf and grabbed the magician again. Randolf threw a punch, but Frank ducked and, bracing himself, shot out his own fist, connecting solidly with Randolf's jaw. Randolf staggered backward but managed to grasp the edge of the disappearing box and pull it down hard on Frank, who dodged left. The box struck Frank only a glancing blow, then smashed at his feet.

Then the magician whipped out more pellets from his pocket. This time he cocked his arm to throw them at Frank's face, but Frank snapped his leg up to unleash a powerful karate kick that caught Randolf by surprise. Frank's foot connected solidly with Randolf's chin, snapping his head backward and knocking him to the ground in a heap.

The crowd jumped to its feet, cheering and whistling. Frank and Joe weren't sure whether the audience thought that this was all part of the show. In any case, the paying spectators seemed satisfied they'd gotten their money's worth.

A short time later, the Hardys, Marlin Randolf, Celina Stiletto, Dr. Greene, and Mickey Barnes were gathered in Barnes's trailer. The police were on their way.

"It was all Marlin's idea," Celina said. "I never meant for anybody to get killed."

She sat in a chair opposite Barnes's desk, with Marlin Randolf in another beside her. Mickey Barnes was in his seat behind the desk, and the Hardys and Dr. Greene stood nearby.

"Why did you do it?" Mickey Barnes asked. "What did you have to gain by killing Bobo?"

"Marlin talked me into it," Celina said. "I just wanted to run away. But he said we had to have money. Then we could leave the show in style and wouldn't have to worry about finding new jobs. And with Bobo's life insurance, we'd have plenty of bucks. All we had to do was make it look like an accident."

"Quiet!" Randolf snapped, shooting to his feet and making a move toward her. Joe stepped forward, placed his hand flat on the magician's chest, and gave a powerful shove that put Randolf back in his seat.

"*You* be quiet," Joe ordered. "You'll have plenty of time to tell your side, too. The police will want to hear it."

"Sounds like you wanted to leave pretty badly," Frank said to Celina.

"Just try living your whole life in a tiny, backwater town like where I grew up," Celina said. "It was so boring, I'd have done anything to get out. So when the circus came through and I met Bobo in town before the show and he gave me a free pass, it was the most exciting thing that had ever happened to me. After the show we met, and we hit it off. He said he could talk Mickey Barnes into giving me a job as a horse groom if I joined, and I didn't stop to think about it but said yes right away. It was a chance to escape the boring life I knew. It would be new

147

and exciting, staying in a different town every night, seeing the country. I didn't even think about it but went straight home, packed a bag, and left.

"At first it was great. Believe it or not, I thought Bobo was charming and cute—and he *was* at first. I let him talk me into marrying him. Then he said I'd make more money if I developed a knife act, so I did." She scowled. "But he just wanted me to support him since he knew he'd be retiring soon.

"Anyway, things changed. *He* changed. How did I know what being married to him would be like? He was always stuffing his face, smoking cigars all day and night, living like a slob—you saw that trailer. I started hating it—hating everything about him. He was always grouchy and criticizing me. He complained I didn't clean up after him, but why should I? I didn't run away from home to be a maid."

"That still didn't give you the right to kill him," Barnes said.

Celina frowned quietly at the floor.

"Where did Randolf come in?" Frank asked.

Celina shrugged. "I needed to talk to *somebody*, didn't I? But Bobo got jealous even when Marlin and I were just friends, so we started sneaking around. We got pretty good at it, and before long we got involved. Finally, we decided to run away. Marlin was tired of show life by then, and I'd had my fill of Bobo. We were going to take off. I was ready to go, but Marlin said we had to have money."

Celina shot Marlin a fierce look. "That's when he came up with his high-wire scheme."

"Celina, stop talking," the magician said. "You're only giving them things to use against us."

But Celina went on. "We didn't find out about Freddie substituting until afterward," she said. "We made sure to be clear on the other side of the grounds when they were rehearsing, just to be as far from the action as possible."

"And the breakaway pin?" Joe asked.

"Randolf sneaked into Freddie's trailer and got the real pin, then during that hour when he knew the breakaway would be with the props near the high wire, he just went into the big top and switched them. But he heard someone coming. He hid the breakaway the first place he saw— inside the other balance pole. Then he rushed out."

"It makes perfect sense, come to think of it," Frank said. "Joe, we should have suspected that whoever stashed the pin in the balance pole wasn't a clown."

"Why should we have assumed that?" Joe asked.

"A clown wouldn't have cared if someone saw him around that area with a juggling pin. Pins are standard clown props. Only a non-clown would be nervous. He'd want to ditch it fast.

That's why he stuck it in the balance pole. It was a panic move."

Frank turned to Celina. "And early on, when Joe and I came by Bobo's and your trailer, asking questions, you told us about Freddie being friends with Behemoth Dan just to send us off in another direction, didn't you?"

She nodded.

"And then when we pressed on," Joe added, "you and Randolf figured you'd better do something to get us out of the way. So you opened the tiger cage when Frank was nearby, and when that didn't work, you put the Gila monster in my bunk."

"Marlin said we had to protect ourselves," Celina said. "You were getting close, and he said we'd go to jail if you found us out."

"Mmm," Joe said. "Tell me, were the tiger and the Gila monster your work or Randolf's—or did you divide the labor?"

"Stop cross-examining her," Randolf said. "You're not the police." He turned to Celina. "Don't say another word."

"I opened the tiger cage," Celina admitted, "but it was Marlin who put the Gila monster in your bunk. I wouldn't touch the lizard. *Ugh.*" She shivered.

"And meanwhile you decided to go ahead and make another attempt on Bobo, didn't you? If at first you don't succeed, as the saying goes," Frank said.

"Marlin said he had a new plan that couldn't miss. It involved chemicals he was going to put in Bobo's makeup. Since chemicals were Marlin's specialty, I figured he was right. It couldn't miss."

Celina shook her head. "Now I'm sorry I ever let him talk me into any of this. The story of my life, right? First I let Bobo talk me into joining up and marrying him, then I let Marlin talk me into this scheme. He mixed the chemicals, and I slipped them into Bobo's whiteface."

There was a moment's silence, then Frank said, "And the whole thing probably would have worked if Joe hadn't noticed that the label on the potato chips bag didn't include garlic as an ingredient."

Dr. Greene cleared her throat. "I guess I owe you two a pretty serious apology," she said to the Hardys.

"Forget it, Doc," Frank said, smiling. "Joe's got a big enough head already. No need to swell it any more. I already know what a good detective I am."

A knock sounded at the trailer door.

"Police," said a deep voice. Two uniformed officers, a man and a woman, came in. When they heard the stories, they snapped handcuffs on Randolf and Stiletto and advised them of their rights. Then they led their prisoners out.

At that point the phone rang.

"Now what?" Barnes said, snatching the receiver. "Yeah?" He listened a moment. "Oh."

His face softened. "Hey, that's great. Did he really? You tell him sure it will. Just as soon as he's ready." The circus boss hung up. "That was Freddie Felix's mother. Great news. He came out of his coma this morning. And guess what the first thing he asked was?"

"If he could have his old job back?" Frank said.

Mickey Barnes stared at Frank. "How'd you know?"

Frank turned to Joe. "It's just as you said—the work's hard, the hours are long, the sleeping accommodations are terrible, and the food's awful. Other than that," he added with a laugh, "it's a great job."

Frank and Joe's next case:

The Hardys are visiting their pal Chet Morton, who's taken a job as a Viking—in a historically authentic village on the Minnesota shores of Lake Superior. The idea is to re-create the bold spirit of the legendary explorers. But someone's out to put on display a more sinister part of the Viking past: the burning, the looting, the terror. The action in Viking Village begins with a few small acts of sabotage, which soon escalate into a full-blown assault. Frank and Joe are ready to meet the challenge—even if it means confronting the cold, hard steel of battle-ax and war hammer. And like true Viking warriors, they know that this fight could be a fight to the death . . . in *The Viking's Revenge*, Case #124 in The Hardy Boys Casefiles™.

Christopher Pike presents....
a frighteningly fun new series for your younger brothers and sisters!

1 The Secret Path   53725-3/$3.50
2 The Howling Ghost   53726-1/$3.50
3 The Haunted Cave   53727-X/$3.50
4 Aliens in the Sky   53728-8/$3.99
5 The Cold People   55064-0/$3.99
6 The Witch's Revenge   55065-9/$3.99
7 The Dark Corner   55066-7/$3.99
8 The Little People   55067-5/$3.99
9 The Wishing Stone   55068-3/$3.99
10 The Wicked Cat   55069-1/$3.99
11 The Deadly Past   55072-1/$3.99
12 The Hidden Beast   55073-X/$3.99
13 The Creature in the Teacher   00261-9/$3.99
14 The Evil House   00262-7/$3.99
15 Invasion of the No-Ones   00263-5/$3.99
16 Time Terror   00264-3/$3.99

A MINSTREL® BOOK

R·L·STINE'S
GHOSTS OF FEAR STREET®

1	Hide and Shriek	52941-2/$3.99
2	Who's Been Sleeping in My Grave?	52942-0/$3.99
3	Attack of the Aqua Apes	52943-9/$3.99
4	Nightmare in 3-D	52944-7/$3.99
5	Stay Away From the Tree House	52945-5/$3.99
6	Eye of the Fortuneteller	52946-3/$3.99
7	Fright Knight	52947-1/$3.99
8	The Ooze	52948-X/$3.99
9	Revenge of the Shadow People	52949-8/$3.99
10	The Bugman Lives	52950-1/$3.99
11	The Boy Who Ate Fear Street	00183-3/$3.99
12	Night of the Werecat	00184-1/$3.99
13	How to be a Vampire	00185-X/$3.99
14	Body Switchers from Outer Space	00186-8/$3.99
15	Fright Christmas	00187-6/$3.99
16	Don't Ever get Sick at Granny's	00188-4/$3.99
17	House of a Thousand Screams	00190-6/$3.99
18	Camp Fear Ghouls	00191-4/$3.99
19	Three Evil Wishes	00189-2/$3.99
20	Spell of the Screaming Jokers	00192-2/$3.99

Simon & Schuster Mail Order
200 Old Tappan Rd., Old Tappan, N.J. 07675
Please send me the books I have checked above. I am enclosing $_____ (please add
$0.75 to cover the postage and handling for each order. Please add appropriate sales
tax). Send check or money order--no cash or C.O.D.'s please. Allow up to six weeks
for delivery. For purchase over $10.00 you may use VISA: card number, expiration
date and customer signature must be included.

POCKET
B O O K S

Name _____

Address _____

City _____ State/Zip _____

VISA Card # _____ Exp.Date _____

Signature _____

1180-16

What's it like to be a Witch?

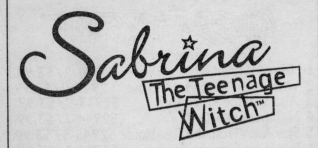

Sabrina The Teenage Witch™

*"I'm 16, I'm a witch,
and I still have to go to school?"*

◆◆◆◆◆

#1 Sabrina, the Teenage Witch
by David Cody Weiss and Bobbi JG Weiss

#2 Showdown at the Mall
by Diana G. Gallagher

Coming in June 1997

Based on the hit ABC-TV series

Look for a new title every other month.

From Archway Paperbacks
Published by Pocket Books

1345